What Do You Do
When Your Mouth
Won't Open?

What Do You Do When Your Mouth Won't Open?

SUSAN BETH PFEFFER

Illustrated by Lorna Tomei

For Joy,
best,
Sue Pfeffer
June 9, 1983

A Yearling Book

Published by
Dell Publishing Co., Inc.
1 Dag Hammarskjold Plaza
New York, New York 10017

Yearling ® TM 913705, Dell Publishing Co., Inc.

ISBN: 0-440-49320-X

Reprinted by arrangement with Delacorte Press

Printed in the United States of America

Second Dell printing—September 1982

CW

For Mildred Lowe
and in memory of
Stanley Lowe

What Do You Do When Your Mouth Won't Open?

Chapter One

IT was 2:15, and Cass Miller was almost through reading her composition. That left just Bobby Morris before I was called on to read, and there were still fifteen minutes left. My only chance would be for Bobby to really mess up, so that the teacher would make him read his composition again and again, until he got it right. That wasn't likely though; Bobby was dumb but he read out loud pretty well, and that meant I was bound to be called on.

All this was Ms. O'Neill's fault, for being sick. Ms. O'Neill was our homeroom and language arts teacher, and she would never have put me in this position. But she had to get sick, so we had this substitute teacher, and she was just going around the room in alphabetical order, making us read our homework assignments, a composition on What We Like Best About Television.

It wasn't like I hadn't done the composition. I had, and it was good, too. I write okay. That wasn't the problem at all.

Cass finished her composition, and the stupid substitute called on Bobby. He started reading his, and I realized his was bound to be short. Bobby never wrote more than two paragraphs in his life; that was all the words he knew. There was going to be enough time for me.

Bobby was finished by 2:18½. At 2:19, the substitute called on me.

"I can't," I said, hoping that would be the end of that. Maybe Ms. O'Neill left instructions.

"Why can't you . . . Reesa?" the substitute asked, after checking on the seating list to see who I was.

"I just can't," I said.

"Haven't you done your homework?" the substitute asked.

I nodded miserably. I was sure I was going to start crying, and that would have been awful. Everybody would have teased me for years if I started crying then.

"Ms. O'Neill doesn't make Reesa read out loud," Heather said. Heather's my best friend, and I should have known I could count on her.

"She doesn't?" the substitute asked. "Is that true, class?"

Everybody in the class answered yes, and things got kind of noisy.

The substitute rapped on the desk with the ruler to get

everybody quiet again. "Why not?" she asked. "Do you stammer, Reesa?"

"No," I said. I still felt like crying. I knew my face was absolutely bright red. I felt like a McIntosh apple.

"Then why don't you have to read out loud?" the substitute asked.

Everybody answered for me again, and the substitute rapped on the desk again. "Quiet, quiet!" she shouted this time. "If I don't have order, I'm going to give all of you extra homework assignments to do."

So everybody got quiet again real fast. And my face got even redder. If everybody ended up with extra homework, they'd all blame me.

"Reesa doesn't have to read out loud because she has a phobia," Laura said.

Laura's this kid with a real big mouth. She tells everybody everything. Sometimes that comes in handy.

"A phobia," the substitute said. "Are you sure you know what that means?"

"It means she's scared to do something," Jenny said. She didn't sound nasty about it, like she sometimes does. Just matter-of-fact. I wished I felt that matter-of-fact, but my face had turned from apple to beet. I had this feeling if the bell didn't ring real fast, my face was going to explode, and there'd be these little pieces of red face splattered all over the kids. I just hoped the biggest piece would land smack on the substitute teacher.

"A lot of people are scared of speaking in public," the substitute teacher said. "But that doesn't mean . . ."

And then the bell rang. Better late than never. All the kids got up and started grabbing books and talking to friends, and I knew I'd been forgotten about.

By everybody except the substitute. "I want Reesa Nathan to stay behind," she called out. I wished I could have pretended not to have heard her, but she really bellowed. She wasn't scared of speaking in public, all right.

So I stayed behind. Heather picked up her books real slow, but when everybody else left the room, the substitute waved her hands to show Heather she should leave too. So Heather did, after looking kind of sorry at me. I smiled back at her. My face was back to apple.

"Come here, Reesa," the substitute said, I wished I could remember her name. She told us in homeroom, but I hadn't paid any attention.

I walked up to her desk, carrying my books with me to show I couldn't stay very long.

"Do you have a bus to catch?" she asked.

"No," I muttered.

"All right, then," she said. "Sit down, Reesa, and tell me about this problem."

"There's no problem," I said, sitting down.

"No?" the substitute asked. "I think not being able to speak in public is a problem."

"I can speak in public," I said. "I'm speaking now, and this is public."

"That isn't what I mean," the substitute said. "How long have you had this . . . phobia?"

"Always," I said.

5

The substitute raised her eyebrows. "Always?"

"Since kindergarten," I said. "I was in this play. I was supposed to be a snow fairy, and I was supposed to say 'I am the snow fairy and I bring the snow' and I rehearsed and rehearsed. I was real little, you know. Only it got to be my turn to give my line, and I couldn't say it. I just stood there, and I started crying, and they had to stop the whole play."

"Terrific," the substitute said. She was older than Ms. O'Neill and not as nice-looking, but she didn't look mean, like some substitutes do. "What happened next?"

"I don't know," I said. "I just cried, I guess."

"No, I mean about your phobia," she said.

"Oh," I said. "Well, I guess I just had it. I was never in another class play again. A couple of my teachers tried. In third grade my teacher told my parents that the only way to cure me was to give me the starring part in the class play, so I'd have to . . . you know, and I knew I couldn't do it, but nobody would listen to me. I was just a kid, so they thought they knew what was best for me. And I learned all my lines and I was the second person to go onstage in the play, and the first kid went on and said all his lines, and then I went on and I couldn't do it. I knew I couldn't, but nobody would listen."

"What happened then?" the substitute asked. "Right then, I mean."

"It's hard to remember," I said. "I think I stood there for a while, and then I started crying again. So the teacher

6

said I didn't have to do the part after all, and she did it for me."

"And that was your last class play," the substitute said. I nodded.

"All right," she said. "A lot of people don't like to be in plays, and things like that. But all I asked you to do was read your composition to the class. Surely you've done that before?"

"I don't have to," I said. "All my teachers know I can't, so they don't make me."

"But you're in seventh grade," she said. "Somebody must have made you read a composition before. Or just read out loud from a story in class."

"No," I said. "Sometimes I had teachers who'd ask me to in the beginning of the year, and I'd explain to them that I can't. And sometimes they don't really believe me, and then they call on me, like in September, and I can't, and they see it. Sometimes they call my parents in then for a conference."

"And what do your parents say?" she asked. I could tell she was really interested. I wished she wasn't.

"My mother says I'll outgrow it. And my father says it isn't all that serious anyway." My older sister, Robby, just thought I was crazy, but I didn't see any reason to tell the substitute that.

"So the teachers don't call on you to read out loud," the substitute said. "And you don't read out loud."

"It's okay," I said. "I get really good marks, so they

7

know I'm not just dumb. It's just something I can't do. Isn't there stuff you can't do?"

"Of course there are things I don't like to do," the substitute said. "But there are things in this life you just have to learn how to do, Reesa. There are fears that have to be conquered. You have to gain control of your own destiny."

"I'm only twelve," I said. "Can't I gain control when I'm a teenager?"

The substitute blushed a little then. "I guess I sounded a little fervent," she said. "But phobias are so terribly crippling, and they're so unnecessary."

"Maybe," I said. "But I have one, and they don't just go away."

"I have a very good friend who had a phobia," the substitute said. "She was scared to leave her house. At first we didn't think it was anything serious, because she wasn't totally honest with us about it. But soon we realized she was terrified to leave her house. She couldn't do anything because she wouldn't go anywhere. One day her daughter got sick, and she couldn't make herself drive the child to the doctor's office. She had to call a friend and ask her to take the baby. It was then that she realized she had a real problem, and that she would have to get professional help. So she went to see a psychologist, and she was in therapy for a while, and now she's perfectly happy and able to go wherever she wants."

"How did she go to the psychologist if she was so scared to leave her house?" I asked.

The substitute pursed her lips. "It wasn't easy for her,"

she said finally. "But that isn't the point. The point is she had a phobia, just like you, and she realized it was an illness, and she cured it with a doctor's help."

"But her problem isn't anything like mine," I said. "Hers was real serious. I'm not scared to do anything important like leave the house. I just can't speak in public. As long as I don't have to do that I'm fine."

"But what about today?" she asked. "When I called on you to read out loud?"

"But that never happens, unless there's a substitute," I said. "Ms. O'Neill never calls on me. She knows better. And if Trudy Mullins hadn't been out sick, you wouldn't have gotten to me and you wouldn't even have known I couldn't do it."

"You're obviously a bright girl," the substitute said. "And you don't seem to be shy. So what do you think will happen to you if you do have to read out loud to a group?"

"I don't know," I said. "I think I'll die."

"You must know you won't really die," she said.

"No, I don't," I said. "I've never read out loud to find out."

"But that's unrealistic to think reading out loud makes you die," the substitute said.

I wanted to say there were a lot of different ways a person could die, but I was starting to feel stubborn. My mother always says it takes a lot to get me mad, but once I am, watch out. I was starting to get mad. This was none of that stupid substitute's business. She wasn't my mother. She wasn't even my teacher, really. I'd never see her again

9

after Ms. O'Neill got back. And she'd already kept me after school for fifteen minutes. So I wasn't about to explain that you could die inside, and it could hurt almost as much as dying outside must. Instead I asked, "What if you're wrong and I'm right and reading out loud would make me die? All it would take would be once, and I'd be dead."

The substitute looked like she was getting mad too. "That's silly," she said. "You're a smart girl and you must know that's just plain silly."

I shrugged my shoulders.

"A very great man once said, 'You have nothing to fear but fear itself,' " the substitute said. "Do you know who said that?"

"Franklin Roosevelt," I said with a sigh.

"That's very good," the substitute said. "How did you know that?"

"Every teacher I've ever had has quoted that to me," I said. "To make me want to speak in public. Every September I hear all about Franklin Roosevelt and how scared he was when he got polio, and how he didn't let himself be scared and became president. May I go now?"

"Just one more minute," she said, and I could see she was angry. Teachers don't like it if you know what they're about to teach you. I don't know why, since it sure could save them time.

I got up anyway, and gathered my books.

"The only person you're hurting with your phobia is yourself," the substitute said. "Nobody else really cares

10

that you won't read in public. It's no one else's loss. Remember that, Reesa."

"I will," I said, and started to leave the classroom. I could feel the substitute staring at me as I left, but that was her problem. Mine was speaking in public, and it didn't bother me one bit that I couldn't. I just wished dumb people like that would leave me alone.

Chapter Two

M S. O'NEILL came back to school the next day, and I was nervous all day long that she'd call me up for a conference about what I said to the substitute. Sure enough, at the end of the day, she did ask me to stay late. I looked sadly at Heather, who gave me a sympathetic look back, and as all the other kids left, I walked up to her desk.

"What's the matter?" Ms. O'Neill asked me. "You look like your dog just died."

"Aren't I in trouble?" I asked.

"No," she said. "Should you be?"

"I don't know," I said. "I just figured if you wanted me to stay late after school . . ."

"Oh, heavens," she said. "It never occurred to you it might be good news?"

"No," I said, starting to feel relieved and kind of excited.

"Well, it is," she said. "You won the school contest on *What I Like Best About America*."

I had to think about that for a second. "I wrote a composition about that," I said. "Ages ago."

"Last month," she said. "It does seem like longer, doesn't it? Anyway, you wrote the essay the judges decided was best in the whole school. I'm very proud of you, Reesa. You were competing against eighth and ninth graders, and yours won."

"Oh, wow," I said. "That's great."

"The next step is the countywide contest," Ms. O'Neill said. "I don't have the details, but Mrs. Perkins does. She wants to see you tomorrow after school."

Mrs. Perkins is the principal. Usually it isn't so great to have her want to see you, but this time it sounded safe. "A county contest?" I asked.

"I'm sorry I don't remember the details," Ms. O'Neill said. "But I'm sure Mrs. Perkins can tell you all about it tomorrow. Tonight you'll just have to enjoy winning the school contest. Congratulations again, Reesa."

"Thank you," I said. Ms. O'Neill stuck her hand out for me to shake, so I did. It felt weird.

I said good-bye to her and ran out of the classroom. Heather was waiting for me.

"Remember that essay we had to write on what we liked best about America?" I asked her.

"Yeah," she said. "It was some kind of a contest."

"Well, I won!" I told her. "I'm the school winner."

"Hey, Reesa, that's terrific," Heather said. She had an enormous smile on her face. Heather never minds when I do something better than she does; that's one of the things I like best about her. Of course I'm not jealous of her, either, when she does better than me on a test.

"Now it goes to the county contest," I said. "Only Ms. O'Neill didn't know the details."

"You're such a good writer," Heather said.

"English is my best subject," I said. I was already starting to think about becoming this really great writer. I'd write novels about kids who were really like kids, instead of the crap they always make us read in school. I thought about that just about all afternoon, even when Heather and I were talking about all kinds of other stuff.

I decided not to tell anybody at home about winning the contest until supper. Every night at supper Dad and Mom ask Robby and me what we did at school that day. Dad used to be the one who asked, but then a couple of years ago, Mom went back to work, so now she asks too. Lots of times I don't have much to tell them, but tonight I knew I had something that would make them really proud of me. So I could hardly wait.

Sure enough, at supper Dad told us about the pictures he had taken for tomorrow's newspaper. Dad's a news photographer, but sometimes he takes pictures of weddings and bar mitzvahs for extra money. Mostly it's just fires and accidents, though. Things can really get grisly at supper; he tells us all about the dead bodies and how he

15

got in real close for a closeup even though the cops didn't want him to. But that's his job, he always says.

Anyway, he hadn't taken many exciting pictures, so he didn't talk very long. Then it was Mom's turn, and she told us all about what happened at the advertising agency. Mom is a copywriter, which means she writes the words in the ads in magazines. She wants to do more than that, but she only got back to it two years ago, so she has a lot of catching up to do.

Words in magazine ads usually aren't too interesting, but Mom always has good stories about the people she works with. People in advertising are crazy, she says, but it's a creative kind of crazy, and she thinks it's fun. I guess it's okay. I miss her a lot less at home than I thought I would.

Then it was Robby's turn. I was hoping she wouldn't have much to say, so I could go sooner, but the one time I had something really important to talk about, there was no shutting her up.

"The most wonderful thing happened to me today," she said. Robby's two years older than me, and she's always been very dramatic.

"What's that?" Dad asked, helping himself to more broccoli.

"Billy Miller asked me out," she said.

Billy Miller is Cass Miller's older brother. Cass says he picks at his pimples when he thinks nobody is looking.

"Billy Miller," Mom said. "Do we know him?"

"Of course you do," Robby said. "His sister Cass is a friend of Reesa's."

"Cass I can picture," Mom said. "How old is Billy?"

"He's my age," Robby said. "You know him, Mom. I went to his bar mitzvah party last year, remember?"

"Oh, yeah," Mom said. "His father is in something silly."

"Swimming pools," Robby said. "Billy hates it. He's going to be a great doctor."

"That's good," Dad said. "You'll never go hungry married to a doctor."

"I'm not going to marry him," Robby said, but her eyes had gotten all dreamy, and I could see she was trying out the name. Robby Miller. She's been doing that sort of thing for the past three years.

"So what are your plans?" Mom said. "For your date, I mean."

"We're going to go to the movies Saturday night," she said. "There's a comedy at the Plaza, and it's PG. We'll go to the early show, and then we'll have ice cream sodas. Okay?"

"Don't forget, you have an eleven o'clock curfew," Mom said.

"We'll be home by then," Robby said. "Promise."

"Will you be going with a group of your friends?" Dad asked.

"No," Robby said. "But a bunch of kids are bound to be going, and we'll probably join them."

I like the way Robby works. She knew Dad would be

happier if she were going on a double date, but she obviously didn't want to do that. So she made it sound like she'd be chaperoned by about twenty kids, without really promising that she would be. There's a lot I can learn from Robby.

"I guess our little girl is growing up," Dad said. He says stuff like that sometimes. "Anything else happen to you in school today, Robby? Something more academic, maybe?"

"I got a ninety on my algebra test," she said.

"That's great," Mom said.

"I should have gotten a ninety-five," Robby said. "I was careless on one question. One thing I just didn't know."

"Ninety is still very good," Dad said. "Better than I ever did in algebra."

"And in my gym today our squad won in basketball," Robby said. "I scored four points. Sheila Morgan scored eighteen points, and Mrs. Morris said she should go try out for the high school team. She said there's real good scholarship money in basketball for girls now. So I've been thinking maybe I should work on my basketball too, and see if I can get a scholarship that way."

"Work on your algebra instead," Dad said.

"Okay," Robby said. She didn't seem to mind.

"So, Reesa," Mom said, "did anything earthshaking happen to you today?"

"To Reesa?" Robby asked, sounding shocked.

"Sort of," I said, and I felt a little embarrassed. I'd been waiting all afternoon to tell, and I just hoped they'd realize how important it was for me.

"Sort of?" Dad asked. "What happened, honey?"

"I won a contest," I said. "It was this schoolwide contest, so I was competing against eighth and ninth graders too, and I won."

"That's terrific," Mom said. "What kind of contest? I don't remember your mentioning a contest."

"It didn't seem very important," I said. "It was an essay contest. I had to write an essay on what I liked best about America. And mine was the best."

"I'm proud of you," Dad said. "I guess she takes after you, Deb. We have another writer on our hands."

"Do you have a copy of your essay?" Mom asked. "I'd love to read it."

"I don't think so," I said. "Ms. O'Neill has it, I guess. She told me Mrs. Perkins would tell me all about the contest tomorrow."

"Did you enter the contest, Robby?" Dad asked. "Reesa said it was schoolwide."

"No, I didn't bother," Robby said. "It was just a dumb contest."

"Will there be some kind of award ceremony?" Mom asked, ignoring her. "Maybe Dad could take the picture for the paper."

"I don't know," I said. I was feeling really good. "But I do know it goes to a county contest next."

"*That* contest?" Robby asked, and for the first time she looked interested.

"Yeah," I said. "What contest?"

"Nothing," she said. "I'm just surprised you entered."

"Why?" I asked.

"Because now you have to read your essay out loud," Robby said.

"What are you talking about?" I asked.

"Didn't they tell you?" she asked.

"No," I said, but I couldn't be sure. I didn't remember much about the contest except writing the essay.

"Each school picks a winner, and then all the winners go to this big assembly and read their compositions," Robby said. "And then they pick the county winner, and then all the county winners go to a state contest. But you definitely have to read your essay at the assembly if you won the school contest."

"I don't believe you," I said.

"Are you calling me a liar?" she asked.

"Now wait a second, girls," Mom said. "Reesa, you didn't know about this?"

"No," I said, real shaky.

"I have the mimeo about it," Robby said. "It's in my room. Can I get it, Mom?"

"Of course," she said. I could tell she was looking kind of worried at Dad.

I followed Robby to her bedroom. I don't know why, since if she said she had the mimeo, she did. For her twelfth birthday, Robby asked for a filing cabinet, and Mom and Dad got her a two-drawer one. It's bright yellow, and it doesn't look like the kind in offices, but Robby likes it anyway. Robby is a very organized person.

We walked over to the cabinet, and Robby opened the

top drawer. She took out a manila folder labeled "Contests" and went through it until she found the paper she wanted.

"There," she said, after she checked it out. She handed it to me triumphantly, so I knew it was bad news.

I didn't want to look at it, because if I did, then it would be true, but Mom and Dad had joined us in the bedroom, so I didn't have much of a choice. Sure enough, it said that the school winner would get to participate in a countywide assembly, to read out loud his or her essay. They made it sound like that was something good.

"Why did you enter?" Robby asked me.

"I didn't know," I said. "I don't think I ever saw this. Ms. O'Neill just told me about the contest, so I wrote something."

"They must not have mimeoed for seventh graders," Robby said. "I guess they figured a seventh grader wouldn't win."

"Well, Reesa sure showed them," Mom said, but she didn't sound too happy about it.

I didn't blame her. What had been perfectly wonderful just a few minutes earlier was now a full-fledged disaster.

"I can't do it," I said, starting to choke up. "I'll drop out."

"Now wait a second," Mom said. "Come on, let's go back to the dining room. We can't talk here."

So the four of us filed back into the dining room. There was still some leftover fish on my plate, but I didn't feel like eating it.

"Now, you know we don't like to give you kids orders," Mom said. "We try to let you make up your own minds on as many things as possible."

I nodded miserably.

"But to throw away an honor like this, because of a silly little phobia," she said. "That would be foolish."

"But it isn't silly," I said. "And it certainly isn't little. Mom, don't make me do it." I tried not to whine, but I was really scared.

"Obviously we aren't going to make you do anything," Dad said. "Especially something like this. It's your honor, so of course it's your decision what to do about it. But you'd really be letting your fear control you, and that's never a good idea."

"But a big assembly," I said. "I'd have to read . . ." I couldn't even finish the sentence.

"I don't think Reesa should have to do it," Robby said. "If it bothers her that much, why should she?"

I wasn't sure I wanted Robby as an ally, but at that point, she was better than nobody.

"Robby, stay out of this," Mom said. Robby looked mad.

"I don't see why . . ." she began, but Dad interrupted her.

"Do me one favor," he said to me. "Don't decide anything tonight. Give yourself a chance to think it over. With an open mind. Then decide. All right?"

"Okay," I said, but I wasn't sure how I could possibly be open-minded about something so awful. Still, it would get Dad and Mom off my back, and that was worth something.

That night I had awful dreams about standing on a stage and everybody charging up at me and throwing things and laughing because I couldn't get my mouth to even open. I knew I'd promised Dad I'd keep an open mind, but I hated the thought of having dreams like that from now on. Or even worse, having those dreams come true someday. As far as I was concerned, I was just going to tell Mrs. Perkins I couldn't do it.

Chapter Three

Ms. O'NEILL didn't make things any easier for me the next day when she announced in homeroom that I'd won the contest. Everybody congratulated me. I tried to smile, but it was as awful as my dream. They'd all laugh at me when they heard I'd turned down winning because of the assembly. But I didn't have any choice.

At lunch, everybody came over to my table. I kept trying to tell Heather what was happening, but we were constantly interrupted. One of the kids who came over was Cass.

"Hey, did you know Billy asked your sister out on a date?" she asked after congratulating me. "He told us this morning at breakfast."

"Robby told us last night," I said.

"Billy can be mean sometimes, but he's okay most of the time," Cass said. "What's Robby like?"

I didn't know what to answer, so I just shrugged my shoulders. "She's okay," I said.

"It'd be pretty funny if they got married," Cass said. "Then we'd be family, sort of."

"I don't think Robby wants to get married until she's finished college and all that."

"Nobody's going to marry Billy until his skin clears up. But it would be funny."

Right then nothing seemed funny to me. "I guess," I said.

"Jenny's waving at me," Cass said. "Congratulations again."

"I thought she'd never go," I said to Heather as soon as Cass had left. "I've got to talk to you."

"Fast," Heather said. "Before somebody else interrupts."

"I have to read my composition at a big assembly," I said. It felt awful just to say it. "And I can't do it. I won't. I'm going to tell Mrs. Perkins that this afternoon. Just drop out. What do you think?"

Heather looked a little puzzled. "Can you?" she asked.

"Sure," I said, but my stomach started churning. It hadn't occurred to me I might not be able to.

"You represent the whole school," she said.

"They can pick the second best composition instead," I said. "That can be the winner."

"But suppose they didn't," Heather said. "They might

26

not have wanted to bother with a second prize. You might just be it."

"Then we just won't have a winner," I said, but I really wasn't happy with the way that sounded.

"Would you do that?" Heather asked. "Keep us from having anybody in the contest?"

"I don't know," I said. I was starting to have an open mind, and I liked that even less than figuring out what I was going to tell everybody about dropping out.

"Maybe Mrs. Perkins will tell you there was a second choice," Heather said. Heather always knows what to say.

"I bet she does," I said, trying to smile. "I guess I'll find out this afternoon."

I didn't pay much attention to school the rest of the day, but it didn't seem to matter. When the bell finally rang, I walked over to the principal's office. Heather came with me.

"My name is Reesa Nathan," I told the secretary. "Mrs. Perkins is expecting me."

The secretary looked at a piece of paper on her desk. "Oh, yes, so she is," she said. "Go on in, Reesa. And congratulations."

"Thanks," I said. Everybody knew. That didn't make me feel any better.

"You must be Reesa," Mrs. Perkins said. We'd never met, but I'd seen her a couple of times at assemblies. She was a middle-aged woman, and she looked pretty nice for a principal. Robby said she was fair. I just hoped she was understanding too.

"Yeah," I said. "I'm Reesa Nathan."

"Congratulations, Reesa," Mrs. Perkins said. "Please sit down."

So I sat in a chair by the side of Mrs. Perkins's chair. I had to twist a little to face her.

"I was one of the judges in the *What I Like Best About America* contest," she said. "And I thought your composition was outstanding. There were several fine essays, but yours really stood out in the crowd."

Just what I didn't want to hear. "Was there a second choice?" I asked.

"We didn't bother with one," Mrs. Perkins said. "After all, we're only supposed to send one student to the county contest, so there was no real reason to come up with a second-prize winner."

"Oh," I said. "I just thought maybe there was another really good one. I'm only in seventh grade, you know."

She looked at me like that didn't make much sense, but I knew what I meant. "You're our first and only choice," she said. "And we handed back all the other compositions to the students' teachers, so it would be close to impossible to come up with a second prize, even if we wanted to. Why? Did one of your friends think maybe she should have come in second?"

"Oh, no," I said. "I was just curious."

"I'm sure you're even more curious about when the county finals are," Mrs. Perkins said. She gave me a really big smile, like I should be jumping up and down, at least inside. I tried to smile back.

"They're two weeks from Friday at the Stanton High

28

School," she said. "Stanton is the county seat, as I'm sure you know. It's a nice big auditorium, and it should be filled to the brim," she said. She sounded really excited about it. "This contest is quite a popular event. I was there last year, and I was very impressed with the quality of the essays. Your competition will be quite fierce."

"Oh," I said. I could picture all the other essay winners looking like saber-toothed tigers.

"There will be a lot of parents there, and teachers," she said. "And each school brings a busload or two of students. There might well be five hundred people there."

Five hundred people. I couldn't have read my essay to my class of twenty-nine, and they expected me to read it to five hundred strangers. That did it. I had to get out of it.

"Friday night," I said. "I don't think I can do it then."

"Oh, dear," Mrs. Perkins said. "There isn't a religious problem, is there?"

"Oh, no," I said. I even had to think for a second to figure out what she meant.

"That's good," she said. "So what's the problem?"

The problem was I didn't have a problem. If I'd thought of it, I would have used religion, but I'd just screwed that one up. And now she thought the problem was it was on a Friday night and it was too embarrassing to tell the truth.

"I . . . My parents work, and sometimes they both have to work late on Friday nights," I said real fast. "My father's a news photographer, and lots of times there are really bad accidents on Friday nights. And murders. Lots of them on Friday nights, and then he has to work late. And my mother . . ." She was tougher, but it felt good to be thinking again. "My mother, well, she's a copywriter, and lots of times Friday is their deadline for their copy, and if she doesn't have it finished by five, she just has to stay in the office and finish it. Lots of times she doesn't get home until really late on Friday, and Dad's taking pictures of murders, or accidents, or robberies—sometimes he covers robberies and they happen all the time on Friday nights—and it's just my sister and me and she's just fourteen, so she can't drive."

Mrs. Perkins stared at me. I think her mouth was even a little open.

"I might not be able to get a ride there," I said. "If my parents are working that night."

"That's no problem," Mrs. Perkins said. "We'll arrange for a lift for you if need be. I can always take you. Don't worry. We'll make sure our prize winner is there to represent Parks Junior High School."

"Oh," I said.

"Now I want you to go home, and practice, practice, practice," Mrs. Perkins said. "How you present your speech will count for fifty percent of the final judging. So no stammering, and no hesitation. Just read those fine words loud and clear and I know we'll all be very proud of you."

I figured if I stammered it would be a miracle, but there was no telling her that.

"Good-bye now, Reesa," she said. "I'll see you two

30

weeks from Friday. And if there are any problems with a lift, just let me know."

I didn't have a choice except to get up and leave, so I did. She'd taken my best and only excuse and found a way around it. It wasn't fair.

"What happened?" Heather asked me as soon as we were safely away from the office.

"I couldn't get out of it," I said. "Oh, Heather, if I have to do it, I'll just die."

"But you have to do it," she said.

"Maybe I could get sick," I said. "Laryngitis. Right before I was supposed to read it. And then you could read for me. You'd do that, wouldn't you?"

"Sure," Heather said, but I could see she wasn't too happy about it. "But doesn't the way you read it count?"

"Fifty percent," I said.

"So if I read it for you, that would be kind of cheating," she said. She didn't look at me when she said it.

"Not really," I said. "Well, kind of maybe."

"Then I really wouldn't want to," she said. "You don't mind, do you Reesa? I just hate cheating. I always get caught when I try, and I wouldn't be any good at all. If you really got laryngitis that would be one thing, but maybe they wouldn't even let you switch; maybe you'd just be disqualified anyway, but at least it wouldn't be cheating. I can't cheat."

I looked at her. "I know you can't."

"So I guess you'll just have to do it," she said. She didn't sound much happier about it than I did.

"Terrific," I said. "I'll do it and I'll just die."

"Maybe you should see a doctor," Heather said. "People with phobias see psychiatrists. Maybe you should see one right now, and he could cure you in time for the contest."

I'd never thought about being cured before. I just figured the phobia was something I'd have to live with for the rest of my life. But then I remembered the story the substitute had told me about her friend. I figured she'd probably made the story up, but that didn't mean it was such a bad idea.

"A psychiatrist," I said. "Well, why not? What do I have to lose?"

Heather smiled at me like she was really proud. And I had to admit, I felt better about the whole rotten thing already.

Chapter Four

MY appointment with Dr. Marks was for 3:00 Friday afternoon. I figured that gave me two weeks to get cured. Besides, that was the first appointment she had available.

Dr. Marks was the only psychologist listed in the Yellow Pages. I'd planned to go see a psychiatrist, but they were listed under "surgeons and physicians," and that sounded medical and kind of scary. Psychologists were close enough. And Dr. Marks was it.

I didn't know what to expect there, but it turned out to be a living room sort of a place, with a sofa and a coffee table and a bunch of magazines to look at while I waited. I read the cartoons in *The New Yorker*; she had four issues there, so there were plenty of cartoons. Before I had to find anything else to read, Dr. Marks came out of her office and told me to come in. She looked a little surprised to see me; I hadn't told her on the phone that I was a kid, and I'd used a real deep voice so I'd sound grown-up.

"Come on in," she said, and she led me to her office. She was kind of pretty, and she looked only a little bit older than Ms. O'Neill. Somehow I'd thought she'd look more like Dr. Spengler, my old pediatrician. But she wasn't wearing a white jacket or anything, just a blazer and a skirt.

Her office had a bunch of framed degrees in it, which I would have liked to look at, but I didn't want to seem rude. Besides, with her the only psychologist in the Yellow Pages, I couldn't afford to be fussy.

"Do your parents know you're here?" Dr. Marks asked me as she showed me where to sit.

"No," I whispered. Usually I'm not too shy, but just then I really felt scared. Maybe she wouldn't see me if my parents didn't know.

"How old are you?" she asked.

"Twelve," I said. "But I'll be thirteen in two months."

"Twelve," she said. "And you came here on your own."

"I figured it was my problem, so I should try to take care of it myself," I said. "My parents love me, but they can't really help."

"How did you know to call me?" she asked.

"You were the only psychologist in the phone book," I said. "And I didn't want to look up anybody under 'surgeons and physicians.' "

"That makes sense," she said. "Well, Reesa, what seems to be the problem?"

"I have a phobia," I said. "And I have to get over it."

"A phobia," she said, looking thoughtful. "What is it you're scared of?"

"Speaking in public," I said.

"A lot of people are afraid of that," she said. "I don't much like doing it myself."

"You don't?" I asked. If she was scared of the same thing I was, she might not be able to cure me.

"It isn't my favorite thing to do," she said. "But I wouldn't say I was phobic about it. Why do you think you are?"

"Because I can't do it," I said, looking down at the floor. "I have awful nightmares about it, and I just know if I actually had to do it, I'd die."

"That certainly sounds like a phobia."

"I told you it was," I said, looking up again.

"Why do you have to get cured now?" she asked.

"I have to read my composition, *What I Like Best About America*, to five hundred people," I said. I nearly started crying, just saying it. "I won this school contest, and now I have to read my composition at Stanton High School. But if I read it, I'll die. I mean," I wailed, "what do you do when your mouth won't open?"

"That is a problem," Dr. Marks said.

"I have two weeks," I said. "That's enough time to cure me, isn't it?"

"Two weeks?" Dr. Marks asked.

35

"And a couple of hours," I said. "I'll come as often as you want, and I promise I'll pay you. How much do you charge?"

"Fifty dollars an hour," she said.

I must have turned green.

"I don't charge for the first consultation," she said. "This visit is on the house, so don't worry about it."

"I'll get a job," I said real fast. "I'll deliver newspapers, and I'll turn over all the money I make to you. Tips too. And I'll pay you back, if you don't mind getting it in sort of dribs and drabs."

"I'd be delighted to get it in dribs and drabs," Dr. Marks said. "But I couldn't possibly cure you in two weeks."

"You couldn't?" I said, kind of shocked.

Dr. Marks sighed. "Phobias are usually deep-seated problems," she said. "With years and years of patterns building up. They aren't just something that you can say 'poof' to and they disappear."

"I'm willing to work," I said. "But I have to get cured."

"It's very good that you're so willing to change your behavior," she said. "That's half the battle, when a person realizes that her behavior is negative, and that it's only hurting herself."

"If that's half the battle, why can't I win the other half in two weeks?" I asked.

"Maybe you can," she said. "But not with my help. I'm a very strict psychoanalyst. Do you know what that means?"

I shook my head.

"Basically it means I think all problems are rooted in childhood trauma. Problems that happened to you when you were a kid."

"But I'm a kid now," I said. "Shouldn't that save time?"

She laughed. "It probably should," she said. "But my patients usually stay with me for two years or more. Even if we cut that in half, it's still a lot longer than two weeks."

"Oh," I said. "So there's no way?"

"There are therapists who believe in much more direct action solutions," she said. "Maybe you should find one of those and get help there."

"But you were the only psychologist in the phone book," I said. "And I can't keep looking around. I only have two weeks."

"I don't know what to tell you," she said. "Except maybe that you have nothing to fear but fear itself."

"I hate Franklin Roosevelt," I said. "What did he know? He wasn't scared of public speaking."

"No, I guess he wasn't," Dr. Marks said. "Good luck, Reesa. I hope you can find a nice quick cure."

Since Dr. Marks got up, I did too. I hadn't been there nearly an hour, but it was free, so I couldn't just stay there if she didn't want me to. Besides, I felt like a dumb little kid. So I left her office and walked home really slowly. It was a long walk, and I had plenty of time to think. Mostly I thought about how much I wanted to be really sick, so I wouldn't have to read my composition in two weeks. If I was practically dead, nobody could expect me to get on that stage and die for them.

So I thought a lot about how to get really sick. I saw a

37

made-for-TV movie once about this group of scientists who were making smallpox or something and they broke a bottle of germs, and they all got sick and nobody knew how for a long time, but the hero figured it all out eventually and they got cured. That sounded real good but if our town only had one psychologist, I didn't think we were likely to have any bottles of smallpox hanging around.

Nobody was home when I got in, so I called Heather and told her about Dr. Marks. She didn't know where to find any smallpox either, but she said her mother had gone to a German measles party once, where a bunch of girls got together because one of them had German measles and that way maybe all of them would get it, and then if they got pregnant later, they wouldn't have to worry about getting it. I told her to let me know if she heard of any parties about two days before I was supposed to speak.

"What's the matter?" Robby asked me when I finally got off the telephone. I hadn't even heard her come in.

"What am I going to do about the contest?" I asked her. I don't usually ask Robby for advice, because she isn't very patient when I do, but I couldn't think of anybody else to turn to.

"If you don't want to do it, don't," she said.

"But I represent the whole junior high school," I said. "I can't let everybody down."

"It won't break anybody's heart if you don't show up," she said. "There was a contest last year and there'll be another one next year. Nobody expects you to win anyway, so what difference does it make?"

"I might win," I said sharply. "Besides, I feel like I have to."

"Then do it and stop complaining," she said. "You're such a crybaby sometimes."

"I am not," I said. "Aren't you scared of things?"

"Sure," she said. "I'm scared some nuclear power plant is going to explode, or maybe we'll go to war, or maybe some crazy person will move to town and murder me. But those are sensible things to be scared of. Not like the stuff that scares you."

"I remember when you used to be scared of thunderstorms," I said. "You'd hide under the bed whenever there was one, and you'd cry like the lightning was going to jump into bed with you."

"I was just a little kid then," she said. "I outgrew it by the time I was ten. Unlike some other people I could mention."

"I'm going to outgrow my phobia too," I said. "In two weeks. Just watch me."

"Sure," she said. "That'll be the day."

I wished I could blame her for her attitude, but secretly I agreed with her. Hadn't Dr. Marks just told me it would take years to get cured? And she was a professional. She knew what she was talking about.

Still, I had a question for Robby. She'd already started reading *Teen Dreams* magazine, but I had to interrupt. "Robby?" I asked.

"What?" she asked, not looking up from the magazine.

"How did you get over being scared of lightning?" I asked.

"I don't know," she said. "It just happened."

"You mean one night there was lightning and you realized you weren't scared anymore?" I asked.

"I guess so," she said. "I really don't remember."

"But you'd been scared of it all those years," I said. "And nothing in particular cured you?"

"I outgrew it," she said. "Like I said before. Being scared of lightning is kid stuff, and I was too old for it. Now leave me alone. You bore me."

"Okay," I said, but Robby gave me something to think about. Maybe I'd just get over my fear like that. Poof—it's gone. I've outgrown it. I was twelve, after all, and I'd be thirteen just a month and a half after the contest. That was much too old for phobias.

I wondered if there was any way of getting mature really fast, but, short of getting married, I couldn't think of any. And there was nobody I really felt like marrying just then.

Suppertime was awful. Even if it was a Friday night, both my parents were there, and they kept going on and on about how proud they were of me because I was going to be in the contest. I'd tried to explain to them that Mrs. Perkins hadn't given me much of a choice in the matter, but I couldn't go into all the details, because they don't like it when they hear that I've sort of lied about them. So they thought I was really terrific, not giving in to my phobia, even though I wanted to give in to it more than anything. And Robby kept interrupting all the time, trying to say something about her algebra class, but Mom and Dad kept talking about me and the contest. Mom wanted to know all about my composition too. "I'm so proud my daughter is a writer like me," Mom said.

That didn't make me feel any better.

We were clearing off the dishes when the telephone rang. Robby ran to answer it. When she came to the dining room, she looked kind of weird.

"It's for you, Reesa," she told me. "It's a doctor. Marks, I think."

"Dr. Marks?" I ran to the kitchen. "Hello?" I said when I picked up the phone.

"Hello, Reesa," Dr. Marks said, and I could hear her smiling. "I did a lot of thinking about your problem after you left. After all, if you're the only psychologist in a town, you have an almost moral obligation to help people even if it goes against your therapeutic training. Do you understand?"

"Sort of," I said. "You want to help."

"Exactly," she said. "So I called up a friend of mine— we were psych majors together, only she went into a whole other way of treating people, much more result-oriented—and she said that lots of people conquer a fear of public speaking in two weeks."

"They do?" I asked.

"They do," she said. "And I went to the library, and there are three books there on how to give a good talk, so

I reserved them in your name. They said they'd hold them for you. Can you get them tomorrow?"

"Sure," I said.

"My friend said a lot of it is relaxation technique," Dr. Marks said. "If you think you could come to my office next Friday at three, I'll teach you a couple of tricks. It really isn't too complicated, and you should learn enough in one session to get you through."

"Thank you," I said. "Oh, thank you, Dr. Marks."

"And it's on the house," she said. "My way for apologizing for being a stuffed shirt."

"You weren't a stuffed shirt," I said. "I'll go to the library first thing tomorrow, and then next Friday I'll go to your office, and thank you. Thank you so much."

"You're welcome," Dr. Marks said. "I'll see you next week."

We hung up then, but I held on to the telephone for a few seconds. "Who was that?" Robby asked. She came into the kitchen with Mom and Dad and they were all looking at me.

"That was Dr. Marks," I said. "She's my psychologist, and she's going to cure me in two weeks so I'll never be scared of public speaking again!"

Chapter Five

I woke up early the next morning, and it drove me crazy waiting for the library to open. Mom suggested I use the time constructively doing my homework, but I was too impatient. I kept looking at the clock instead, waiting for it to be 10:00. Finally, at 9:55, I figured it was okay to bike over to the library; by the time I got there it would be open.

I would have asked Robby if there was anything she wanted, but she was still asleep. I had to tiptoe all morning long, so I wouldn't wake her. That only made me jumpier.

I got to the library at 10:02, and sure enough it was open for business. I parked my bike outside and went in. I've been to the library a thousand times, but I always go to the children's section. Dr. Marks hadn't said so, but I figured the books she'd reserved for me were in the adult part.

So I went up to the main desk and said, "My name is Reesa Nathan, and there are some books reserved for me?" I didn't want it to, but it came out sounding like a question.

The librarian looked at a list. "*The Art of Public Speaking, How to Be an Effective Public Speaker*, and *Stand Up and Speak Out!*?" she asked me.

"I guess so," I said. "I know they're about public speaking."

"Then these must be them," she said. "You going to give a speech?"

"Yeah," I said, waiting for my stomach to lurch the way it always did whenever I thought about it. But it didn't. At least not as much as it usually did.

"With the help of these books, you should certainly be a success," she said.

I gave her my library card, and she checked the books out for me. It was real easy, and I decided 'f they didn't mind kids taking out adult books, I'd come back and take out some dirty ones.

I didn't have time then, though. Instead I got back on my bike and rode home in record time. As soon as I got in, I charged up the stairs, waving the books at Mom and Dad.

"Hey, you woke me!" Robby called from her room.

"Sorry," I said, going into mine. I closed the door behind me, so if I made any noise turning the pages, Robby wouldn't hear. She can be really fussy when you wake her.

I spent the morning looking over *The Art of Public Speaking*, hoping it would tell me all kinds of secret ways to success, but it was pretty boring. The print was small, and a lot of it was how to give a good business talk. You were supposed to start with a funny story and then go into all the statistics. None of that mattered to me, since I had my speech all ready, and there weren't any statistics in it.

So I put it down and picked up *How to Be an Effective Public Speaker*, but that wasn't any better. By the time I went downstairs for lunch, I was discouraged, afraid that Dr. Marks had picked out the three worst books, and I'd never learn how to do it, and I'd go onstage and I wouldn't even have statistics come out of my mouth. It was a depressing thought.

Saturday lunches we all make do for ourselves, so Mom and Dad were both out when I finally went downstairs. Robby was in the kitchen, though, making a late breakfast.

"How's it going?" she asked me as she scrambled her eggs.

"Okay," I said, checking out the refrigerator. I tried to look busy, so she'd stop asking me questions.

"I figured by now you'd be a pro," Robby said, and turned the heat off. She put her eggs on a plate and sat down at the kitchen table. "Did those books you got help?"

"They're helping," I lied. I didn't want **H**
how bad things were going. It wasn't just **H**
I didn't want anyone to know how scared
again.

"If you need help . . ." Robby said, and **E**
eled a forkful of scrambled eggs into her
you know."

"I'm okay," I said sharply. I ended up g
of salami and taking it back to my room. T
the world I needed right then was Robby'
less she was ready to write a book about p
that could really teach me something.

But as I ate my salami, I found Robby
write anything for me. *Stand Up and S*
third of the books Dr. Marks had reserved f
what I'd been dreaming about. It was fun
could understand what it was talking abou
me all kinds of sensible suggestions about h
surviving a talk in public. It even said it wa
scared to speak in public.

I'd never known that before. Finding o
only one who panicked made me feel bette
so weird.

The book had a whole list of helpful
problem was that the first helpful hint wa
yourself with what you were going to read
over and over again. That was when I rea
gotten my composition back from Ms. O'Ne
out the original ages ago, so I didn't have
with. And I could hardly remember what I'

46

wouldn't hear. She can be really fussy when you wake her.

I spent the morning looking over *The Art of Public Speaking*, hoping it would tell me all kinds of secret ways to success, but it was pretty boring. The print was small, and a lot of it was how to give a good business talk. You were supposed to start with a funny story and then go into all the statistics. None of that mattered to me, since I had my speech all ready, and there weren't any statistics in it.

So I put it down and picked up *How to Be an Effective Public Speaker*, but that wasn't any better. By the time I went downstairs for lunch, I was discouraged, afraid that Dr. Marks had picked out the three worst books, and I'd never learn how to do it, and I'd go onstage and I wouldn't even have statistics come out of my mouth. It was a depressing thought.

Saturday lunches we all make do for ourselves, so Mom and Dad were both out when I finally went downstairs. Robby was in the kitchen, though, making a late breakfast.

"How's it going?" she asked me as she scrambled her eggs.

"Okay," I said, checking out the refrigerator. I tried to look busy, so she'd stop asking me questions.

"I figured by now you'd be a pro," Robby said, and turned the heat off. She put her eggs on a plate and sat down at the kitchen table. "Did those books you got help?"

45

"They're helping," I lied. I didn't want Robby to know how bad things were going. It wasn't just Robby, though. I didn't want anyone to know how scared I was getting again.

"If you need help . . ." Robby said, and then she shoveled a forkful of scrambled eggs into her mouth. "Well, you know."

"I'm okay," I said sharply. I ended up grabbing a hunk of salami and taking it back to my room. The last thing in the world I needed right then was Robby's help. Not unless she was ready to write a book about public speaking that could really teach me something.

But as I ate my salami, I found Robby didn't have to write anything for me. *Stand Up and Speak Out!*, the third of the books Dr. Marks had reserved for me, was just what I'd been dreaming about. It was fun to read, and I could understand what it was talking about, and it gave me all kinds of sensible suggestions about how to go about surviving a talk in public. It even said it was normal to be scared to speak in public.

I'd never known that before. Finding out I wasn't the only one who panicked made me feel better, like I wasn't so weird.

The book had a whole list of helpful hints, but the problem was that the first helpful hint was to familiarize yourself with what you were going to read, by reading it over and over again. That was when I realized I'd never gotten my composition back from Ms. O'Neill. I'd thrown out the original ages ago, so I didn't have a copy to work with. And I could hardly remember what I'd written.

46

So I figured I'd practice by reading something else out loud. The book said that was a good idea, to get you familiar with the way your voice sounded when you made a speech. It even had a copy of the Gettysburg Address to practice with. It was a terrific book.

"Four score and seven years ago . . ." I began, only I giggled, so I had to stop and start all over again. "Four score and seven years ago . . ."

"What're you doing?" Robby asked. She just opened the door and asked, right when I was in the middle of "seven years ago."

"I'm reading the Gettysburg Address," I said.

"Why?" she asked.

"Because I don't have my composition," I said. "And this book says to read something to get the feeling of it."

"Want me to listen?" she asked. "I don't have anything better to do."

"No, that's okay," I said. "I think the first few times I read it, I should do it alone."

"How about later?" Robby asked. "If I'm not busy, I mean."

"No," I said. Just the thought of reading out loud to someone made my stomach hurt.

"Don't read the Gettysburg Address too much," Robby said. "It could be dangerous."

"Why?" I asked.

"What if when you're supposed to read your composition you freeze and all that comes out is 'Four score and seven years ago'? That could happen, you know."

"It won't," I said. "This book says to use the Gettysburg Address, so I will. This is a very good book."

"I think you're crazy," Robby said. "Are you going to read the Gettysburg Address all afternoon?"

"If I have to," I said.

"Don't when Billy gets here, okay?" she asked. "I don't want him to know I have a crazy sister."

"Okay," I said. "Now would you please leave me alone? The book says I should spend a lot of time reading out loud just by myself. Just to get a feel for it."

"I think you should get a feel for the loony bin," Robby said, but she closed the door and left. And I went back to the Gettysburg Address.

By suppertime I had read the Gettysburg Address seventy-nine times out loud, and I was starting to worry that Robby might be right and that would be what came out of my mouth at the contest. I certainly knew it by heart. The book said the more you read your speech, the more familiar with it you'd be and the less you'd have to read the actual speech, so you'd look more at ease, more conversational. It said giving a speech was just like having a conversation when the other person just said "uhm" a lot. They were there, but they were letting you do all the talking. I wondered if Abraham Lincoln had read the Gettysburg Address seventy-nine times before he actually delivered his speech. Then I thought maybe he'd read my speech seventy-nine times instead, and I started giggling. That was when I knew I was punchy, and it was a good thing it was time for supper.

"I could certainly hear some kind of activity up in your room," Dad said after we'd all served ourselves. "What were you doing up there, Reesa?"

"I was reading the Gettysburg Address," I said, wolfing down some mashed potatoes.

"I'll say she did," Robby said. "That was all I could hear all afternoon long."

"You mean it drowned out those records of yours?" Dad asked. "The age of miracles truly hasn't passed."

"I told Reesa not to read the Gettysburg Address when Billy is here," Robby said. "I want her to behave herself, Mom."

"I'm sure Reesa will," Mom said. "How's it going, Reesa?"

"Terrific," I said. "*Stand Up and Speak Out!* is the most wonderful book ever written."

"Better than Shakespeare?" Robby asked.

"Let Reesa finish, Robby," Dad said, taking some more mashed potatoes and pouring gravy on them.

The mashed potatoes made me think of something in the book. "Mom, the day of the contest, I can't have any supper. Okay? Don't try to make me eat."

"I never knew I force-fed you," Mom said.

"You don't," I said. "But I don't want you to even try."

"All right," she said. "But why not?"

"Because in *Stand Up and Speak Out!* it says that it's real bad to give a speech on a full stomach," I said. "It says that even if you eat something mild and settling for the stomach, like mashed potatoes even, just having to

50

give the speech could make you sick to your stomach, and then instead of giving your talk you could end up throwing up mashed potatoes and gravy all over everybody."

"Reesa!" Robby said. "That's disgusting."

"But that's what the book said," I said. "And I don't want to throw up when I have to give my speech. I'll never win if I throw up right on stage. Maybe even into the audience. Somebody in *Stand Up and Speak Out!* did that, and he had to practically commit suicide, he was so embarrassed."

"Mom, make her stop," Robby said. "I'm going to throw up if she doesn't."

"I think that's enough talk about throwing up," Dad said, pushing his plate away from him. He still had lots of mashed potatoes on it, too, but Mom didn't look like she was going to say anything about being wasteful. Actually she looked kind of green.

"So I won't have to eat supper?" I asked Mom.

"I may never feed you again," she said. "I may never feed anybody again."

"If I hear one word about throwing up when Billy gets here I'll kill you," Robby said to me.

"Okay," I said. It wasn't my favorite topic either, really. So instead I started telling everybody all about *Stand Up and Speak Out!* and all the great advice in it. Robby made a big point of clearing off the dishes, to show she wasn't interested, but I didn't care. Just talking about the book even just to Mom and Dad made it feel more real to me, like I was actually going to give that speech and not die.

Just like *Stand Up and Speak Out!* said I would. And even though Robby would walk back into the dining room occasionally and yawn really obviously when Mom and Dad weren't looking, she didn't make me feel bad.

Billy showed up right on time, and Dad let him in. We were all in the living room, except for Robby, who was upstairs putting on her makeup. Mom and Dad don't let her wear much, but it takes her hours to put on the little they let her.

I checked Billy's skin out first. He did have a couple of pimples, but who doesn't? I'd been expecting smallpox like in that movie.

Robby came downstairs like a princess in blue jeans. Billy said hello to her, but then he turned to me.

"Cass told me about that contest you won," he said to me. "Congratulations, Reesa."

"We're all very proud of Reesa," Dad said.

"Do you think you'll go to the contest?" I asked Billy. "It's two weeks from Friday."

"Why would Billy want to waste his time with that?" Robby asked, getting her jacket. "Come on, Billy, we don't want to miss the movie."

"Okay," Billy said, but he turned to me and said "Congratulations again" before they left. That made me feel really good.

"He seems like a nice boy," Mom said after they were gone.

Dad nodded. "Very polite," he said. "Not the kind of boy to throw up on a date."

52

Mom laughed but I didn't say anything. He was a lot nicer than Cass ever made him sound. But then again, people probably thought Robby was nicer than I did. Brothers and sisters are always nicer to the rest of the world than they are to you.

Chapter Six

MONDAY morning I made a point of asking Ms. O'Neill for my composition back. She thought it was pretty funny she'd never given it back to me, and I agreed with her. But I didn't tell her about the Gettysburg Address, which I now could practically recite backward.

When I got home from school that afternoon, I took my composition and read it to myself silently a few times. *Stand Up and Speak Out!* recommended that, to let you get familiar with what you were going to say.

It was a pretty good composition, and I felt proud knowing it was the best one at my school. But after I'd read it five times, I was impatient to start reading it out loud.

I followed the book's directions again. First I read the composition out loud without trying to sound impressive, just to hear what the words sounded like. I did that a couple of times. Then I moved over to my full-length mirror and read the composition out loud in front of it a few times. At first I just read it, but then I practiced looking up from the paper and making eye contact. Of course I was making eye contact with myself, and that felt pretty silly, but that was what the book told me to do.

Robby walked by my room at one point and looked in on me reading to the mirror. "You get stranger and stranger," she said, but that was all she said, so I figured I was getting off lucky and continued telling the mirror what I liked best about America.

Then I went back to reading the composition to an audience, which now consisted of my favorite teddy bear and Amanda, my best doll, the only one I couldn't bear to give up when I outgrew dolls last year. I sat them down in different parts of the room and read the speech out loud again six times. By that point I was nearly as sick of it as the Gettysburg Address, even if I had written it. So I was almost glad when Robby came in.

"I could hear the silence," she said. "You through for the day?"

"For a while," I said. "Could you hear how I sounded?"

"I wasn't really listening," she said. "Why? Are you ready for a live audience?"

"Oh, no," I said, and I was surprised how the thought of having a real live person hear me upset me.

"You'll have to be at some point," she said. "There won't be five hundred teddy bears out there, you know."

"I know," I said. "And *Stand Up and Speak Out!* says I

should read my speech out loud to people before I do it in public."

"I'm here if you want," Robby said.

"No, thanks," I said. Robby was the last person I wanted as my audience. The book said you should have people who'd only say good things about you to hear you read the first few times. And Robby hadn't said anything good about me since I'd stopped using diapers.

"I think I'll ask Heather to come over tomorrow," I said. "She can be my audience."

"But she won't tell you what's wrong with you," Robby said. "Heather always thinks whatever you do is terrific."

"I know," I said. "And when I'm ready for serious criticism, I'll know who to ask." Jack the Ripper would be a better choice than Robby, but I didn't dare tell her that. "But right now all I want is someone who'll just listen and applaud. That's what the book says I should have."

"I'm so sick of that book," Robby said. "You'd think that was the only book you ever read."

"It's the most important one," I said. "It's changing my life."

"I only wish it would change your personality," Robby said. She picked up the book, glanced at it, and tossed it on my bed. "If you ever want an honest opinion, you know where to find me."

"Robby," I said as she started to leave.

"Yeah," she said, turning around to face me.

"Do you really want me to do well in the contest?" I asked.

"Sure," she said. "Why not?" And she left the room before I had a chance to answer.

I read my composition out loud to Teddy and Amanda two more times, and then I quit to do some homework before supper. The speech was sounding good, and I was sure Heather would like it when I read it to her the next day.

Heather agreed to come over as soon as I asked her, and we went home right after school. I was scared to have a human being to read it to, but it was only Heather, and I felt pretty good about how well I could read it. I'd read it a lot the day before, and I knew lots of good stuff about eye contact.

Robby wasn't in when we got home, which made me feel better. We would have gone to Heather's house, but she has an older sister and a younger one, and her mother doesn't have a job, so her house is always full of people, and I wanted to be as alone as possible. Heather's mother might walk in and want to listen, and I knew I wasn't ready for that yet. I wasn't even ready for my own mother. So it had to be my house.

We went straight to my bedroom. I set up Teddy and Amanda in different corners, and put Heather in the center of the room. I figured since she was human, it was best to have her there. Then I read the composition to myself a couple of times, to remind me of how it sounded, like the book told me to. And then I started.

"I've always known I was lucky to be born an American," I began. But I knew I wasn't looking up the way I

was supposed to. My eyes were glued to the paper. "I've got to start again," I told Heather. "I'm sorry."

"That's okay," she said. "Take your time."

I love Heather. I took a couple of minutes and read the essay to myself again. This time I was so familiar with it, I knew I'd be able to look up. So I began again.

"I've always known I was lucky to be born an American," I said, looking straight ahead. Way over Heather's head, to the wall behind my bed. If we'd been in the auditorium, I'd be looking at the doors, like all I wanted to do was get out.

"I'm not doing it right," I said. "I have to start again."

"It's hard to get it right the first time," Heather said. "That's why I'm here."

"I'll do it right this time," I said. "Just watch." I looked down at the paper, like maybe I'd forgotten what it said, and then started again. "I've always known I was lucky to be born an American," I said. I held my head up and looked at Heather, but it wasn't like a normal conversation. It was like she was in the audience somewhere, just the way she was supposed to be. I could see her smile at me, so I figured I should go on to the second sentence. "Although my grandparents were born in the United States, their parents weren't, and they've told me many stories of how life was in the old country, and why it was so important for them to leave and seek a new life in the United States." Whew. That was a long one, and I managed just fine. Heather was still smiling, so I turned my head slightly and faced Teddy. "They didn't have much

60

money, and they had to work very hard and live in tenements, but they never regretted leaving." I was fine, but in the corner of my eye, I could see Heather was fighting off a giggle.

"What is it?" I asked. "Am I doing something wrong?"

"Oh, no," Heather said, only now she was really laughing.

"Come on," I said. "What am I doing wrong?"

"Nothing," she said. "Only you looked so sincere talking to the teddy bear like that. Like he really cared about your grandparents."

"Great-grandparents," I said, but that only got her laughing harder. "How about if I look at the doll instead?" I asked.

Heather started rolling around on the floor waving her hands around. I got really mad for a minute, but then I couldn't help it, and I started laughing too. I must have looked pretty dumb giving this serious speech to a teddy bear. And poor Heather, sitting in the middle of the room, between Teddy and Amanda, trying to keep from laughing. It really was silly.

Of course right then Robby had to come on upstairs. There we were, looking like total fools, and in she walked. She looked at both of us and shrugged her shoulders.

"I should have known," she said. "There's no way you're going to be able to handle the contest, Reesa. No way at all. I just wish I didn't have to be there to be thoroughly embarrassed by you."

That made me stop laughing. It took Heather a second

or two longer, but she stopped too. We both stared at Robby.

"I guess you think this is one big joke," she said. "But if you could hear the way Mom and Dad go on and on about how proud they are of you, you wouldn't be wasting your time laughing yourself sick."

I opened my mouth. There weren't any words to come out.

"If all you intend to do is make a fool of yourself, I wish you'd just drop out," Robby said. "And not drag Mom and Dad and me all the way over to Stanton to see you stand on stage and laugh like some kind of idiot. Sometimes I think you'll never grow up."

"You stop that, Robby," Heather said.

"All right," Robby said. "But you're as bad as she is. Encouraging her to do something she can't possibly do." And she walked away from my doorway. I could hear her go to her room and slam the door behind her.

Heather got up and closed my door. "How can you let her get away with that?" she asked me.

"I don't know," I said. I was feeling awful, like everything Robby said was true.

"I'd never let Alison talk to me like that," Heather said.

"Yeah, but Alison is different," I said. "She isn't mean like Robby."

Heather shook her head. "I'm sorry," she said. "It was my fault we were laughing like that. I got us started."

"Maybe this isn't such a good idea," I said.

"My being here?" Heather asked.

"No, all of it," I said. "Maybe I'm just kidding myself,

and I will make a fool of myself, like I did in third grade. That would be so awful."

"You're not going to do that," Heather said. "You're going to be absolutely terrific."

"How do you know?" I asked. "How can anybody know?"

"I know because I know what kind of person you are," Heather said. "You're not a quitter."

"I've never had the chance to quit before," I said.

"And you don't have the chance to now," she said. "So you're going to read your composition and you're going to win that stupid contest. I know you will, and if you know you will also, you will. You know?"

"I guess so," I said. I was waiting for Heather to say, "You have nothing to fear but fear itself," but she didn't. I guess that's one of those things only adults say.

"Heather?" I asked.

"Yeah," she said.

"What if I can't?"

"I don't even hear you," she said. "Now read me your stupid speech, all right?"

"All right," I said, and I read it out loud. I didn't care about lifting my eyes off the paper, or addressing different parts of the audience. I just read it, and when I was finished, Heather clapped and clapped, and demanded that I read it again.

I read it to her five times, and by the fifth time, I was hardly looking at the paper; I was looking around the room, talking to her and Teddy and Amanda like they were the world's biggest audience. At the end of each reading Heather clapped, and by the fifth reading, I felt like clapping too.

I would have read it to Heather another five times after that, but I knew that wouldn't be fair, so we went downstairs and had a couple of oranges. Heather left just as Mom came in.

"How are you, honey?" Mom asked me as she took off her jacket. "Did you have a good time with Heather?"

"Fine," I said. "I read her my composition."

"Reesa, that's great!" she said. "I bet Heather was a wonderful audience."

"She was," I said. "Mom, I have to go upstairs now, and practice some more."

"Of course, honey," she said. "But before you go, I want you to know how very proud of you your father and I are. Not just because your composition won, but because you're doing something we know is very difficult for you."

"Thanks, Mom," I said. She kissed me on the cheek as I walked past her. I hoped she couldn't see the tears in my eyes.

Sure Heather had been a great audience, and sure Mom and Dad were proud of me. But Heather hadn't been able to answer my question. What would happen if I got onstage and just couldn't do it? What if I froze like I used to? What if I died? Would Mom and Dad be proud of me then?

And even if they could forgive me, could I ever forgive myself?

Chapter Seven

E VEN though I knew I should have found live audiences to practice my speech on on Wednesday and Thursday, I limited myself to Teddy and Amanda. I didn't want to think what the authors of *Stand Up and Speak Out!* would think of me, but I couldn't help it. I just wasn't ready to find another way I might goof up.

So I was really impatient for Friday to come and for my appointment with Dr. Marks. I wondered if she'd been thinking about me all week long. At my worst point, Wednesday night before I fell asleep, I was convinced she'd forgotten all about me, and had scheduled somebody else, somebody who'd pay her, for 3:00 on Friday. It took me a long time to fall asleep that night.

Friday eventually came, and even though some of the kids asked me to go with them to the candy shop, I told them I couldn't. I ran all the way to Dr. Marks's office and got there ten minutes early, so I reread all the cartoons in *The New Yorker*s. Even though I'd forgotten most of them, they weren't as funny the second time around.

"Reesa," Dr. Marks said promptly at three. "It's good to see you again."

"Thank you," I said, and followed her into her office. "And thanks for seeing me, and for those books you reserved for me."

"Are they any help?" she asked as we sat down.

"Oh, yeah," I said. "Especially *Stand Up and Speak Out!* I've gotten a lot out of that one."

"So you've been practicing hard?" she asked.

"Every day," I said. "I just about know my composition by heart, even though the book says I don't have to, just as long as I feel familiar with it."

"And have you read it out loud to an audience yet?" she asked.

"Sort of," I said. "Mostly to my doll and my teddy bear, but my friend Heather came over on Tuesday, and I read it five times to her."

"Not bad," she said. "How did it feel?"

"Scary at first," I said. "But by the end it was okay."

"You don't sound too happy about it," she said.

"I'm still scared," I said. "Oh, Dr. Marks, I'm so scared it scares me. What if I can't do it? My mom and dad are so proud of me, just because I'm trying, but I'm sure I'll get onstage and freeze. What happens then?"

"Your parents will still love you and be proud of you," Dr. Marks said. "I can just about guarantee that."

"But it would be so awful," I said.

"It wouldn't be great," she said. "So why don't we see what we can do to keep that from happening?"

"But I want to talk about what will happen if it all goes bad," I said.

Dr. Marks sighed. "If we were doing the sort of therapy I usually do, I'd encourage you to talk about it. Endlessly. But we aren't, and I checked with my friend, and she says the worst thing we can do is dwell on how things could go wrong. Sure you could freeze. The building might also collapse in an earthquake. The idea isn't to prepare for those disasters but to assume they won't happen, and to work to see that they don't. The way you've been practicing all week with your speech, the way the book told you. Are you still with me?"

"I shouldn't think about failing," I said slowly.

"That's it exactly," she said. "Think about succeeding instead. It's called self-fulfilling prophecy. If you think of yourself standing there not being able to speak, that may well happen. But if you think of yourself on that stage, reading your composition clearly and proudly, then that's what'll happen."

I thought about both pictures. I liked the successful one a lot better.

"As a matter of fact, one of the exercises I have for you is for you to picture yourself on that stage, reading your composition all the way through, and everybody applauding once you've finished," Dr. Marks said. "And I want you to think about that picture—the whole scene—every night before you fall asleep. If you have time to in the morning, picture it then, too, when you wake up. And if you start to have bad fantasies, fantasies about failing, just refuse to think them. Switch over to the good fantasy immediately. Do you think you can do that?"

I nodded. It sounded easy enough.

Dr. Marks smiled. "The rest of what I have to teach you is fun stuff," she said. "Just a couple of relaxation techniques. I use them myself at times; they're helpful to know."

"I'm ready," I said.

"All right," she said. "This is another fantasy one. I use it when I'm standing in line at the bank and slowly growing crazy. All you have to do is close your eyes, like this, and relax your shoulders, and start picturing yourself in the most relaxing place you know. The place where you're happiest. Do you have a place like that?"

"My grandparents' house," I said. "Their kitchen. My grandmother loves to cook, and the room always smells so good, so warm."

"Terrific," Dr. Marks said. "Perfect. Now close your eyes and picture yourself in that kitchen. Everything smells so good, and you can just feel all the love."

So I tried it. It felt pretty good.

"You see how easy that is," Dr. Marks said after a moment. "It's a great way of escaping pressures."

"When should I use it?" I asked her.

"Anytime you think you can't deal with where you are," she said. "If you find when you're waiting for your turn to speak that you can't stand being where you are, that you think you'll scream if you have to wait any longer, then close your eyes, and transport yourself to your grandmother's kitchen. Like I say, I do it all the time when I'm standing in lines. I hate standing in lines."

I smiled at her. "Okay," I said. "What's next?"

"Deep breathing," she said. "I told you these were easy. Deep breathing is a well-known relaxant."

"You mean I should just breathe deeply when I feel tense?" I asked.

"Basically," she said. "Try to take ten deep breaths, and hold them for a beat of ten before you exhale. Exhale slowly too. Come on, let's practice together."

So we breathed deeply for a while. It did make me feel a lot more relaxed about things.

"When do I do that?" I asked.

"I do it when I have to go to the dentist," Dr. Marks said. "I always get tense when I have a dentist appointment, and that helps me. All it does is calm you down. I'd do it as close to when I was supposed to speak as possible. Maybe when the speaker before you is on."

"Grandma's kitchen and deep breathing," I said. "This is terrific. It's as good as the book."

"I'm glad to hear it," Dr. Marks said. "Are you ready for one final one?"

"Sure," I said.

"This one is kind of a giggle," she said. "My friend taught it to me last night."

I could picture Dr. Marks and her friend working on these things together last night, and it made me feel really good. Kind of important.

"The idea is to relax every part of your body," Dr.

Marks said. "You start with your head, close your eyes, I guess, and make sure your forehead isn't wrinkled. Then relax your neck, and your shoulders, and then your chest."

"How?" I asked. This was an awful lot of relaxing.

"Try a couple of deep breaths," she said. "Then rotate your head, and shake your arms and jiggle your legs. End up with your feet and toes. Wiggle your toes in your shoes. Here, watch me."

She got up and gave me a demonstration. She looked pretty silly, breathing and jiggling with her eyes closed, like she was trying to shake off something she didn't want to see.

"I know," she said, opening her eyes and joining me in laughing. "I look like I have St. Vitus's dance. My friend can do it and you can hardly see that she's doing it, but she says that takes practice. Come on, get up and give it a shot. Once you get over feeling silly, you'll see it really does relax you."

So I got up and breathed and jiggled, and it did feel good. Tingly and alive.

"But if I do that, everybody will see me and laugh," I said. "I don't think I have time to practice doing it so nobody'll see."

"So everybody sees," Dr. Marks said. "You don't care what the other contestants think, do you?"

"No, I guess not," I said. I'd never really thought about them.

"Let me tell you something," Dr. Marks said. "I know you're going to be terrific next Friday night. But I also

70

know you'll feel a little stage fright. You wouldn't be normal if you didn't."

I nodded. *Stand Up and Speak Out!* said the same thing.

"The thing is, there won't be a kid there who won't be feeling stage fright too," she said. "Some of them will be in much worse shape than you because you've been working all this time to do your best possible job. Some of those kids won't even have looked at their essays in the past two weeks. Showboats. And a lot of them will be like you used to be, scared of public speaking. Maybe not to the degree you've suffered, but they'll be scared, and they won't know how to handle it. They won't have seen me for help. They won't have read *Stand Up and Speak Out!*"

I thought about that, and I knew she was right. I was better prepared.

"So if you want to stand backstage and jiggle your entire body, sure you might look a little funny," Dr. Marks said. "But there'll be kids there who'll be envying you because you know what to do to relax yourself. Because you've put care and thought into what you're doing. And they won't be laughing. They'll be cursing themselves out."

I closed my eyes and pictured that. I was backstage, feeling really cool and jiggling away, while everybody else was whispering, "Gee, I wish I knew how to do that." I giggled.

"All right," Dr. Marks said. "Maybe I got a little vehement there. But I'm just so impressed with you, Reesa, and what you're doing for yourself, that I know you're going to be a big success at it. And I want you to know that too."

"I think I do," I said.

"I don't suppose you have a copy of your essay on you," she said.

"Yeah," I said. "I made a copy, so I could take it to school with me and read it whenever I have a free moment. To get completely familiar with it."

"How about reading it to me right now?" she asked.

"Oh, I can't," I said. "I've only read it to Heather and my dolls."

"You're going to have to read it to somebody else sometime," she said. "We could have a little practice session. Start with Grandma's kitchen, and end up with deep breaths. Then you could read me the composition, and see how it all feels together."

"But what if I can't?" I asked.

"We aren't going to worry about that," Dr. Marks said. "We both know you can. So how about it?"

"All right," I said, but I could feel my stomach starting to ache.

Dr. Marks gave me a long hard look and she said, "Grandma's kitchen." So I forced myself to close my eyes and relax my shoulders and picture myself there. Grandma was baking bread, and it was so warm there. The sun was shining through the windows, and Grandy was sitting at the table drinking coffee and complaining about the Yankees. It felt so good to be there.

"Jiggle!" Dr. Marks said, so I kept my eyes closed, and

rotated my neck and jiggled my body, my arms and legs and toes, and breathed deeply, until my body felt really good, and my stomach wasn't so clenched up.

"Now ten deep breaths," Dr. Marks said, and I breathed deeply, counting to ten with each breath and exhaling slowly to the count of ten. By the time I finished, a truck could have hit me and I wouldn't have cared.

"Are you ready?" she asked.

"Ready," I said. "Only I have to get my composition out of my notebook."

Dr. Marks laughed. "Get it out, and then breathe five more times," she said.

So I did what she told me. I held the composition while I took my five last deep breaths, and that felt good, having it with me.

"Now," Dr. Marks said.

"I've always known I was lucky to be born an American," I began, and I read the whole thing all the way through, looking up a lot at Dr. Marks, and not giggling once, or freezing, or coming close to dying. I just did it, and when I finished Dr. Marks clapped, and then hugged me.

"Reesa Nathan Superstar!" she cried out.

And I felt like one too.

Chapter Eight

ROBBY had another date with Billy Saturday night, so I decided that would be a good time to rehearse my speech in front of Mom and Dad. I'd never done it with two people before, but I knew I'd have to, and they seemed like my best choices.

The only problem was that after reading the essay out loud to my doll and teddy bear all afternoon long, I got impatient. So I waited until Robby was upstairs taking a shower, and then I went downstairs, gathered Mom and Dad, and asked them if they'd mind listening to my speech.

"We won't mind at all," Dad said, sounding very happy.

So I sat him and Mom down. Then I jiggled my body. I had to explain what I was doing, since it did look pretty silly, but they agreed that it was a good technique. Then I breathed deeply, until I felt really relaxed, and when I knew I was ready, I read my composition.

I didn't flub once. I looked up from the paper a lot, and looked at both of them and never felt like giggling or freezing. I just did it, the same as I had with Dr. Marks. And it felt so good.

"That's wonderful," Mom said. "Oh, Reesa, we're so proud of you."

"If you don't win first prize, I don't know who will," Dad said. He took out his handkerchief and blew his nose. It never occurred to me that listening to my essay would make anybody cry. I kind of liked it.

"Read it again," Mom said. "I want to hear it again."

"Yes," Dad said. "Please, Reesa. One more time."

"Okay," I said. I'd read it five times for Heather, after all. So I started all over, only without the jiggling. I did some deep breathing, though; that seemed like a good habit to keep.

I was halfway through when Robby came downstairs. "Oh, is this the famous speech?"

"You've heard it before," I said, losing my place.

"Only through walls," she said. "I've never been invited."

"You're invited now," Mom said. "Sit down and listen to your sister. She's really very good."

"No," I said. "I'm not ready for Robby to hear me yet."

"That's okay," Robby said. "I don't want to hear your dumb speech anyway."

"Girls," Dad said, but the doorbell rang, and he got up

76

to answer it. "Hi, Billy," he said. "Come on in. Robby's all ready for you."

"Robby, we'll discuss this later," Mom said.

"We will not," Robby said. "We'll discuss it right now. I'm sick and tired of the way you keep fussing about Reesa, like it's the most amazing thing in the world that she's willing to open her mouth in public. It's a stupid talk, and she's never going to win anything, and you both know it."

"Hi, Robby," Billy said. He was standing in the entryway to the living room, looking awfully embarrassed.

"Let's go," Robby said.

"Don't stay out too late," Dad said. "We're going to have a talk when you get back."

"I don't have anything more to say," Robby said. She went to the closet and got her jacket, and then she and Billy left.

"Well," Dad said. "The joys of teenage daughters."

"We are going to have to talk to her," Mom said.

"No," I said. "Not on my account. Please."

"But, Reesa—" Mom said.

"It's okay," I said. "Robby has to listen to me read my speech over and over again. She must be sick of it. I don't blame her for not wanting to hear it again. Don't get mad at her."

"That isn't it, honey," Dad said. "It's the way she put you down. Your composition is terrific, and I think you're going to win. It makes me angry when your sister doesn't support you too."

I couldn't figure out any way of explaining to Dad that I could win the Nobel prize and swim the English Channel and be the first person on Mars and Robby would still put me down. So I just shrugged my shoulders.

"It seems to me Robby interrupted your speech," Mom said. "How about starting from the beginning? I would like to hear it again. And then when you're finished, we could all go out for pizza. How does that sound?"

"Terrific," Dad said. "Reesa?"

"All right," I said. "I have to jiggle."

"Jiggle away," Dad said, so I did. Then I breathed, and then I read my composition. I wasn't as good this time as I had been the first time, but I managed to get all the way through. And I think I felt a little less scared when I did it.

Saturday nights I get to stay up late, but I didn't want to be up when Robby got back from her date, so I went to bed early. Besides, all that jiggling was pretty tiring. I wasn't asleep when Robby came in, but whatever she said to Mom and Dad, nobody shouted, so I guess it wasn't too bad. I was asleep by the time Robby went to bed, so I couldn't tell whether she was putting some kind of curse on me. She used to do that when I was really little, and it always scared me.

I tried to keep my distance from Robby the next day. It wasn't hard in the morning, since she slept until eleven. After she woke up I went upstairs and did my homework. I had plenty of it. I stayed upstairs until I heard her come back up, and then I went downstairs and made myself lunch. I went back to my room then, and worked some more. But I made a point of not looking at my composition, because I was afraid if I did, I'd want to read it aloud, and that might drive Robby crazy. So I stuck to math and history.

I was starting to go a little crazy by the afternoon, and it felt silly to be holed up avoiding Robby when, as far as I knew, she wasn't mad at me. Maybe at Mom and Dad, but not at me. I wanted to get out, watch some TV, go for a walk, call Heather, do something. So I decided I could, but first I had to read my speech. Just once, but enough so I could know a day hadn't gone by without my doing it.

I decided I wouldn't read it real loud though, just mutter it. I was in the middle of muttering the second paragraph when somebody knocked on my door.

"Come in," I said.

It was Robby. "Hi," she said. "What're you doing?"

"Nothing," I said. "Junk."

Robby came into my room. "I'm sorry about last night," she said, sitting down.

"That's okay," I said. "You must be sick of this speech."

"Kind of," she said. "How's it coming?"

"Pretty good," I said. "I was just doing it now."

"Oh," she said. "I didn't mean to interrupt."

"Did you have a nice date last night?" I asked. I wanted to change the subject before Robby asked if I'd give the talk for her. I wasn't sure she would, but there was always a chance Mom and Dad told her to. And I still wasn't ready for her honest criticisms. I was pretty sure I wouldn't be ready until about two weeks after the contest.

"It was okay," she said. "We went to the movies."

"What did you see?" I asked.

"Some dumb comedy," she said. "*Big Bellies*. Billy thought it was funny, but I just thought it was dumb."

"Oh," I said.

"So how's it going?" she asked.

"What do you mean?" I asked.

"Your speech," she said. "How are you doing?"

"It's okay," I said nervously. Why was it the only time Robby wanted to talk about me, I wanted to talk about anything else?

"Did you feel comfortable doing it with Mom and Dad?" Robby asked.

"Yeah," I said. "Dr. Marks taught me all these relaxation techniques, and I did them and they helped. They look pretty silly, but I'll do them backstage before I give my talk on Friday, and they should help. Dr. Marks is really nice."

"Do you want to do your talk for me?" Robby said. "I promise I won't be mean."

"I don't think so," I said. "You've heard it anyway."

"I know," she said. "I just thought you might like a fresh audience."

"Maybe later this week," I said. "Wednesday or Thursday."

"Okay," she said. She looked like she was about to get up, but she sat back down. "Tell me, has all this helped you in school?"

"What?" I asked. "I'm doing okay in school."

"I don't mean your grades," she said. "I mean reading out loud. Are you doing that now?"

"You mean like class participation?" I asked.

"Yeah," she said. "All that stuff you've always been too scared to do. Reading your compositions, and reading out loud. Are you doing that stuff now?"

"No," I said. "It hadn't occurred to me to."

Robby giggled. "Well, don't you think it should have?" she asked.

"I guess so," I said. I'd never thought about that, about talking up in class like everybody else.

"If you read your speech in front of five hundred people, your teachers aren't going to let you get away with not reading in class," Robby said. "Nobody'll believe you have a phobia anymore."

"That's because I won't," I said. "It'll be like you and the thunder. I'll have gotten over it."

"It seems to me it might be easier for you to start now," she said. "First you read your speech to Heather, and then to Dr. Marks, and then to Mom and Dad. Maybe you should try reading it in front of an even bigger group before you do it in front of five hundred strangers."

"You mean I should read my speech to my class?" I asked. "I don't know if they'd want to listen. Or if Ms. O'Neill would let me."

"It doesn't have to be your speech," Robby said. "But I bet at some point during school there'll be something to read out loud. Don't you think it would be good practice for you to do it?"

I thought about it. Robby had a point. It was silly to go

from two people to five hundred without anything in the middle. And if I could read something in class, I'd sure be able to read my speech at the contest. It would just mean ending my phobia a little earlier, a little less dramatically.

But if I did it, I'd know I didn't have a phobia anymore, and then I wouldn't have to worry about the speech at all. And *Stand Up and Speak Out!* said you should look for as many opportunities as possible to practice your public speaking.

"Maybe you're right," I said. "Maybe it would be a good idea."

"I think so," Robby said. "I just want you to know I have been thinking about you, Reesa, about how to help. Maybe it doesn't always seem that way, but I really do want to help."

"I know," I said. "And I appreciate it. Thanks, Robby."

"Let me know how it goes tomorrow," she said, getting up to leave.

"Tomorrow!" I said. "You think I should read out loud tomorrow?"

"There's no point waiting," Robby said. "The sooner you do it the sooner it'll be done."

"Yeah," I said, knowing she was right. If I wasn't going to wait until Friday to put an end to my phobia, then there was no reason not to do it tomorrow.

So why did I feel like the world was going to end?

Chapter Nine

I didn't tell anybody my plan to read out loud in class because I wasn't sure I'd have a chance to anyway, and besides, I didn't want anyone to know in case I chickened out. I didn't plan to, but phobias are funny things, and I wasn't sure I could count on mine being really dead. So I kept my plans to myself.

I was starting to grow a little crazy when there weren't any chances to try out my new willingness to speak in public, but then we finally had our language arts class, and Ms. O'Neill announced that we were all going to read a story out loud.

"It's a story with a lot of dialogue," she said. "And I want you to see how it sounds to have a different one of you reading each character's part. Like it was a play.

After all, the junior high school play is going to be having its auditions in a couple of weeks, and I know there are some budding actors in this room who'd like to get in some practice in dramatic readings."

This was my chance! I just knew it. I only hoped Ms. O'Neill asked for volunteers.

She did. "All right. Raise your hands, any of you who are interested in reading parts in this story."

A bunch of hands went up. I almost couldn't lift mine, but then it shot right up, like it knew all along what I wanted to do.

I don't think Ms. O'Neill even saw me, since she was so used to my refusing to do stuff like that. She was calling out names, and there weren't many parts left. I was getting desperate.

"Ms. O'Neill!" I called out, like I had to go to the bathroom really fierce. "Can I read?"

"Reesa?" Ms. O'Neill said.

"Can I read, please?" I begged.

"Good heavens," she said. "I mean, of course you can. I'm delighted. Are you sure?"

"Yeah," I said. "I've been practicing for the contest on Friday, and I'm over my phobia and everything."

"Wonderful," she said. "That's great news. Of course you can read. You be Anne, all right?"

"Okay," I said, and started skimming over the story to see how many lines Anne had. She didn't have too many, but that was okay. I didn't think Ms. O'Neill was ready for the shock of me playing a starring role.

Ms. O'Neill finished casting the story, and then we began reading it. Laura was reading the parts that weren't dialogue, and a lot of the other kids had parts. There were a lot of characters in the story, so we all had to pay attention to see when we were supposed to read. Anne didn't show up until near the end of page two, so that gave me plenty of time to breathe deeply. I would have loved to jiggle, but I couldn't see getting up to do it in the middle of class. Besides, I would have lost my place and missed my cue. So I just sat there and breathed, and tried to think about how impressed everybody was going to be when I read Anne's dialogue. They'd probably insist I try out for the school play. And maybe I would too, if I felt like it.

By the time we reached the middle of page two, my heart was beating really fast. I figured at first that was because I was so eager to read out loud. But then it started pounding and all I could think was "I won't be able to do this," and there was no time to slip into Grandma's kitchen. I was sweating too, and all of a sudden I wanted to throw up. I tried to remember what *Stand Up and Speak Out!* said to do then, but all I could remember was not to eat heavily, and that made me want to giggle wildly and not stop.

" 'Let's see what Anne thinks,' " Bobby Morris read.

That was my cue. I was supposed to say "I think that's a good idea." My lips were really dry. I ran my tongue over them, and tried breathing deeply, but nothing would come out.

" 'Let's see what Anne thinks,' " Ms. O'Neill read, to encourage me.

I was getting very dizzy, and I was sure I was about to throw up all over everybody.

"Anne?" Ms. O'Neill said.

I'd never fainted before, but I was sure I was about to. It would have been a relief.

"Reesa," Ms. O'Neill said. She sounded concerned. "Reesa, are you all right?"

"No," I said. At least my mouth said no. I don't think the word came out, I was holding on to the desk tightly, praying I would die on the spot.

"Do you want to see the nurse?" Ms. O'Neill said. "You don't look well, Reesa."

"Oh, it's just her stupid phobia," one of the kids said. I was feeling too rotten to check to see who said it.

"I do not have a phobia," I said. That did come out, loud and clear.

"Then read your line," the kid said. I think it was Tommy Higgins, but I didn't think I had the strength to find out.

"She doesn't have to if she doesn't want to," Heather said.

"I want to," I said. "I can. I don't have a phobia anymore."

"All right," Ms. O'Neill said. "Bobby, would you read your last line?"

" 'Let's see what Anne thinks,' " Bobby read.

I tried to find my line, but I couldn't locate it. The

words were starting to swim around on the page. "I've lost my place," I said.

"Sure." I was positive it was Tommy.

"Bottom of the page, Reesa," Ms. O'Neill said. "You're supposed to say 'I think that's a good idea.' "

" 'I think that's a good idea,' " I repeated. I still couldn't find my place, so I just said what Ms. O'Neill told me to.

Everybody clapped, like I'd just done something wonderful.

"Sure," Tommy said. "But she won't be able to say her next line. Anybody want to bet?"

"Tommy, you're not helping matters any," Ms. O'Neill said.

"She's holding us all up," Tommy said. "It isn't fair."

I could feel myself blushing. I just hoped no one else could see me.

"That's enough, Tommy," Ms. O'Neill said. "Come on, Laura, it's your turn. Let's get this show on the road."

So Laura went back to reading. My next line was on the middle of page three. I read along with the rest of the class, but I kept looking over to my line. I was sure if I was familiar with what I had to say, it would help.

This time Jenny came before me. " 'Anne, do you have the money?' " she asked.

All I was supposed to say was "I have a dollar." That's all. I say that all the time in real life. But knowing that didn't help. I couldn't say anything. I just shook my head.

"All right, class," Ms. O'Neill said, and slammed her

book closed. "I don't think this has been such a good idea, after all. Why don't we spend the rest of the class with a little spelling bee."

"That's not fair," Tommy said. "The rest of us were doing really good. It was all Reesa's fault."

"Tommy!" Ms. O'Neill exploded. "All right, that does it. Forget the spelling bee. We'll have a little surprise quiz instead. Take out a piece of paper, everybody, and we'll see how well you can spell."

"I'm sorry," I said. "It is all my fault."

Ms. O'Neill sighed. "It isn't anybody's fault," she said. "And I shouldn't be giving you a quiz just because I lost my temper. Besides, at this point, there isn't enough time. So why don't we all just read quietly from our books until the bell rings."

Everybody looked relieved. Everybody except me, that is. I tried to finish reading the story, but I was working too hard at not crying. Everything I'd worked so hard on, all that breathing, all those readings of my composition, and I still had my phobia. It wasn't gone. If I had it on Monday, I was sure to have it on Friday as well. I'd never be rid of it; I was crazy to think I ever would be. And what happened today would be mild compared to what I'd go through on Friday when I'd be standing in front of five hundred strangers, debating whether to faint or throw up or both. No matter what Dr. Marks said, I couldn't do it. I might as well just return *Stand Up and Speak Out!* to the library; maybe somebody else could really use it.

Eventually the bell rang. We all got our books together. I was scared Ms. O'Neill would want to keep me after school, to give me a pep talk and maybe tell me about Franklin Roosevelt, but she just waved us all out of the classroom. That was the only good thing that had happened.

"It's okay, Reesa," Heather said. "Just think of it as a setback."

"Thanks," I said. I just wanted to go home and cry. "I'm okay."

"I know that," she said. "I've heard you read out loud. You're terrific and you're going to be great on Friday. Just you wait and see."

"I'm all right!" I snapped at her. "Now would you just stop it!"

"I'll stop it, all right!" Heather snapped right back. "I'll stop listening to your dumb speech and telling you how great you are, too, if you want."

"Heather!" I cried.

"I'm sorry," she said, and she looked awful, guilty and sad.

"No, I am," I said. "I just feel rotten."

"It's okay," she said. "And it isn't a dumb speech. It's a very good speech."

I was glad Heather could forgive me, since none of this was her fault. As far as I could see, it was all mine, and the only person I had any right to be angry at was me. That just made me hate myself even more.

Heather and I were walking out of the building, not saying anything, when Cass caught up with us. "Hi," she said. "I'm sorry about what happened in class."

"It's okay," I said.

"That Tommy is such a big mouth," she said. "He has no discretion."

"I wanted to hit him," Heather said. "I'm surprised Ms. O'Neill didn't keep him after school."

"It wasn't his fault," I said miserably. "He was just telling the truth."

"He didn't have to tell it the way he did," Heather said.

"He didn't have to tell it at all," Cass said.

"Thanks," I said. It was good to have friends.

"Hey, isn't it weird about Billy and your sister?" Cass asked. I got the feeling she said it just to say something.

"What about them?" I asked. Any topic was better than thinking about what an awful failure I was.

"How they split up," Cass said.

"You didn't tell me they split up," Heather said to me.

"I didn't know," I said.

"Yeah," Cass said. "Billy said he didn't like the way Robby was always putting Reesa down. He said that was all she ever talked about, and he really didn't like it."

"Oh," I said.

"Billy is always teasing me," Cass said. "Robby must have really been something if it was too much for him."

"Robby's been in a bad mood lately," I said.

"Robby's been awful lately," Heather said. "I don't know how Reesa manages to put up with her."

"She isn't so bad," I said, but I had stopped paying attention. I was thinking instead about the conversation Robby and I had had yesterday. The one where Robby had told me to read out loud in school, to make sure I could do it before Friday. The one where she kept urging me to do it, kept saying what a good idea it was. The one we'd had the day after she'd been so mean about me, so mean that Billy had split up with her. That mean rotten miserable two-timing conversation.

"Hey, Reesa, where are you going?" Heather called after me. I hadn't even realized it, but I'd started running away from her and Cass.

"I'm going home!" I shouted back.

"What's the hurry?" Heather cried, trying to catch up with me.

So I slowed up just long enough to tell her. "I'm going home to kill my sister!" I screamed. "Do you hear me? I'm going to kill her!"

Chapter Ten

I ran all the way to the house, got the house key out with shaking fingers, and ran straight upstairs to Robby's bedroom. She wasn't there.

So I started screaming "Robby! ROBBY!!" but she didn't answer.

She wasn't home.

That made me even madder. I was sure she'd run away, so that she'd never have to face me. Just vanished, disappeared. The only reason I had any doubts was because I knew she'd want to hear all about my disaster in school; it was unlike her to miss an opportunity to hear how awful my life was. Thanks to her. And she wasn't even home for me to kill her.

I knew I had to do something. I stood in her room, with

everything in perfect order, the way she always kept it, and I knew if I didn't do something I'd go crazy.

Something made me walk over to her filing cabinet. I opened the top drawer and started taking files out, just one at first, then handfuls of them, and took the papers out of each manila file, and started throwing them all over the room, scattering them like confetti. When I'd finished with the first drawer, I opened the bottom one, and pulled those files out too, and filled the air again with all of Robby's precious pieces of paper. Files and pages floated around all over the room, on her chest of drawers, her bed, her desk, all over the floor. Hundreds of pieces of paper—the room was white now, and you couldn't see the furniture for the paper.

"What are you doing?"

I whirled around and saw Robby. She must have come in while I was going through her file cabinet; I'd been having too good a time to listen for her.

"Getting even," I said, and I took the manila folder I was holding and tore it in half. It was empty, so I could do it easily. Then I threw both pieces at Robby's face.

First she just looked shocked. Then she walked over to me and slapped me really hard.

So I started crying. What I would have liked to have done was slap her back, but I'd wanted to cry for so long, that just happened first.

"This is horrible," Robby said, looking around her bedroom. Then she started crying too. "Why did you do this, Reesa? What did I ever do to you?"

94

That got me mad again, but I was crying too hard to shout. "You know what you did," I choked out.

"I didn't do anything," Robby said, only it was hard to understand what she was saying because she was crying. We were both sobbing, standing there, surrounded by all the mess. I thought I should feel better seeing Robby so miserable, but it didn't help much. I just wanted to kill her a little less.

So I inhaled real hard, figuring it would give me the advantage if I got to speak first. "You know what you did," I said.

"I don't know what you're talking about," Robby said, also inhaling deeply. "Why did you destroy everything?"

"I didn't destroy anything," I said. "Except that one folder. I just scattered things around."

"I'll say," Robby said, and then she almost giggled. Not quite, but close.

So I almost smiled. "I'll help you pick up," I said, and started gathering the pages together.

"No," Robby said. "You'll get everything out of order."

That did make me smile. Robby looked like she was going to start crying again, but she just sighed.

"Okay," she said. "Let's pick everything up, and then I'll sort everything out later."

So we started gathering the pages together, not talking at first. We put them in two piles that kept getting higher and higher. Robby looked at the piles at one point and started crying again. It was all I could do to keep from going over and hugging her. But it was all her fault, after all, and I wasn't about to comfort her.

"Okay," she said when all the papers were in piles. "I can straighten them out now."

"I'm not leaving," I said.

"What are you going to do?" she asked. "Take the papers and start throwing them around again?"

"If I have to," I said.

"How would you like it if I did that to your room?" she asked. "Just took all your private possessions and started flinging them around? How would that make you feel?"

"No more rotten than how you made me feel today," I said.

"I didn't do anything to you today," Robby said. "I haven't even seen you since breakfast."

"It's what you did to me yesterday," I said. "Remember?"

Robby looked like she was really thinking about it. "Yesterday?" she finally said.

"Yesterday," I said. "When you practically ordered me to read out loud in school today."

"Oh, yeah," Robby said. "How did that go?"

I nearly hit her. "You know exactly how that went," I said. "You had it all figured out when you suggested it to me."

"Wait a second," Robby said.

"You knew I wouldn't be able to do it," I said. "You knew I'd choke up, just like always. You knew I'd fail. That's why you told me to do it. Admit it, Robby. You were mad because Billy split up with you. Because of how nasty you've been to me, and you decided to get back at me. You knew just what to do to make me fail and feel

97

rotten and insecure and you did it. And I hate you. Do you hear me. I hate you!"

"Oh," Robby said.

"Is that all you can say?" I shrieked. " 'Oh?' "

"I'm sorry," she said. "I thought you'd do really well today."

"What are you talking about?" I said. "You knew I'd fail. You knew it all along."

"I did not," she said. "You've been seeing that psychologist, and all you ever seem to do nowadays is read that stupid speech and jiggle and show off. I figured you'd be fine in school today."

I looked at her very carefully. She didn't sound like she was lying. "If you thought I'd be able to do it, why did you tell me to do it, then?" I asked.

"Did it ever occur to you I thought it might be a good idea?" Robby asked. She sounded like she was about to cry again. "That I thought it would be good for you to have some practice reading out loud before a big group before Friday? I don't suppose you ever thought of that."

"No," I said. "You haven't exactly been nice to me lately, Robby. You haven't had my best interests close to your heart. So why the switch?"

"Because of Billy," she said. "Because of what he said. Can we sit down?"

"Yeah, I guess so," I said, so we walked over to her bed and sat down together.

"What did Billy say?" I asked.

"He said he thought I was real immature the way I kept

98

putting you down," Robby said. "He said it was one thing to insult a kid sister—he does that all the time—but it was something else to really be mean and rough to her. The way I was to you. He said he didn't want to see me anymore because of how I was with you."

"I'm sorry," I said.

"Yeah," she said. "Only it really isn't your fault. At first I thought it was. I was really mad at you Saturday night because every time I offered to help you, you've turned me down, but then I could hardly sleep and I thought about it, and I realized I have been awful to you lately. Not that you haven't deserved a lot of it. But not all. Some of it I did because I was hurt, but mostly because I was jealous of you. The way Mom thinks you're a great writer. I'm better than you in math, but that doesn't seem to count. I get jealous of you a lot, Reesa. Almost all the time sometimes."

"Really?" I said. "I know you haven't been happy lately, but you get jealous of me other times too?" I felt a little dense for not noticing anything about Robby except how mean she'd been.

"Sure," she said. "I guess I've been jealous of you since you were born. Mom says I was. You were always so cute. You're cuter than me, you know."

"You're prettier," I said. "And you get to wear make-up."

"But you'll get to wear makeup too," she said. "And your nose is smaller than mine."

"But I've always been jealous of you," I said.

"Sure," she said. "Because I'm older, and I get to do more stuff. And believe me, I let you know about as much of it as possible, to keep you jealous. But Mom and Dad always pay more attention to you."

"You mean because of the contest?" I asked.

"Now, yeah," Robby said. "And before that there was your phobia. I always figured you did that just to get attention."

"I did not," I said, but I realized I wasn't sure.

"Whatever," Robby said. "In any event, you've always had things better than me."

"Yeah?" I said, marveling at all the stuff I had to learn. "Like what?"

"Like your name," Robby said. "You have such a pretty name. Not like mine. Roberta. Yuck. All my life the boys have called me Robert. 'Hey, Robert.' I hate it. And I don't think it's fair you got such a pretty name when I came first. They should have started with Reesa and then hit Roberta."

"It isn't easy being named Reesa," I said. "I always wanted a cute nickname like yours. Robby. Only I'd spell it with an 'i.' But you can't call me Reesi. That's ridiculous."

"Robby isn't bad," Robby said. "With an 'i,' huh?"

"That's how I'd spell it," I said. "Besides, the boys always call me Reese's Peanut Butter Cups."

"But I can never fall in love with anybody named Robert," Robby said. "Robert and Roberta. Or what if his last name is Roberts? I could never go through life named Roberta Roberts. I'd die first."

"I could never marry PeeWee Reese," I said. "Reesa Reese is even worse than Roberta Roberts."

Robby giggled. "It is," she said. "Just a little."

"I guess we could keep our own names," I said. "They can be Roberts and Reese and we'll just stick to Nathan. Nathan isn't so bad."

"I suppose," she sighed. "How about Robby with just one 'b' and an 'i'?"

"Write it out," I said, so she found a blank piece of paper and wrote it. Robi. It looked pretty good.

"I like it that way," I said. "It looks French."

"Maybe I'll spell it that way from now on," she said. "Thanks, Reesa."

"You're welcome," I said.

"Was it really awful for you today?" she asked. I could tell she wasn't being mean about it either. Just concerned.

"Yeah," I said. "I froze just like I used to. I don't know what I'm going to do about Friday." I wanted to start crying again.

"You're going to be great on Friday," Robby said. "There's no comparison."

"How can you say that?" I asked. "You were the one who said it would help me to read out loud in class."

"I was wrong, obviously," Robby said. "It's like Daddy."

"What about him?" I asked.

"You know what he always says," Robby said. "That he takes his best pictures when they're really important ones. Murders and big accidents."

"Fires," I said.

"He loves fires," Robby said. "That's it exactly. When the pressure is on him, he does his best work. And the pictures he takes of city council meetings and the mayor giving a speech don't come out nearly as well."

"And you think I'm like that?" I asked.

"Well, you're not like Mom," Robby said. "Mom would give speeches standing in line at the bank if they'd let her."

I giggled. "Dad hates giving speeches," I said.

"I know," Robby said. "I practically begged him to give one on being a photographer for career day last year. That's a really exciting job, you know, and I knew the kids would want to hear about it. Mom kept offering, but being a copywriter just isn't as interesting. Dad only agreed to do it when I said he'd do it for you because he loves you more. That usually works."

"You're kidding," I said.

"No," she said. "I'm not sure if it's true, but it seems to be a good way to get him to do stuff for me."

"Gee," I said.

"Anyway, I bet you work best under pressure too," Robby said. "And today just wasn't exciting enough for you. You had to get your adrenaline pumped up for your first performance. And once that's out of the way, you'll be just great."

"Thank you," I said. "I hope you're right."

"I hope I am too," Robby said. "Because if I'm not, you'll probably come back here Friday night and destroy my room again and Mom and Dad'll blame me and I'll end up getting punished. So you'd better be good Friday, or I'll kill you."

"Okay," I said, wanting to be convinced that she was right. "I'll be good on Friday."

"Oh, who cares," Robby said. "Be great on Friday. Rub my nose in it."

We both smiled. "Can I help you with your files?" I asked.

"No, thanks," Robby said. "You've been more than enough help."

"I'm sorry," I said. "I was mad."

"No kidding," she said. "There is something you can do for me, though."

"What?" I asked.

"Would you read your composition to me?" she asked. "It's kind of hurt that you haven't wanted to yet."

"Oh," I said. "Oh, of course I'll read it to you. Stay there and I'll get my copy."

And when I came back to her room, she was sitting right where I'd left her, waiting to be my audience.

She was a terrific one too.

Chapter Eleven

FRIDAY had to come eventually.

For all my squawking to Mrs. Perkins, Dad drove Mom, Robby, Heather, and me to Stanton High School that night. Dad said there could be a triple murder and the biggest fire in the history of the county, and he still wouldn't have missed the contest. Mom didn't say anything about Friday deadlines because I'd made that part up. I didn't do too much talking on the way over, but it didn't matter because everybody else was talking for me. I think they were all as nervous as I was.

When we got to the school, I saw Mrs. Perkins was already there. She waved me over, and I left everybody else to join her. My heart was already thumping.

"Reesa, this is Mr. Sanchez," she said. "Mr. Sanchez is the principal of Stanton High School."

"Hi," I croaked. I sure hoped I could talk louder than that onstage.

"Hi, Reesa," Mr. Sanchez said. "If you want to join the other contestants, they're backstage." He pointed to the right of the stage.

"Thank you," I said. "I think I will."

"Reesa has a lovely speech to give," Mrs. Perkins said. "We're very proud of her."

"Thank you," I said.

"Tell me, Reesa, was there any problem getting a lift over here?" she asked.

"Oh, no," I said. "No big fires tonight."

"Good," she said. "Well, best of luck. I know you'll do right by Parks Junior High."

"I'll try," I said. I shook Mr. Sanchez's hand as he wished me luck and made my way backstage.

As soon as I got there, I knew I wanted to be home. The panic just swept over me. I tried to calm myself by looking around, and I saw one girl sitting in a corner crying. That made me feel a little better; I hadn't gotten to that stage yet.

And then I decided I wasn't going to. A lot of stuff about phobias was letting them know who was boss. And Dr. Marks had certainly taught me techniques for when I wanted to be someplace else. So I closed my eyes, and rotated my head, and thought about my grandmother's kitchen.

It was warm in there, from the oven being on, and Grandma was baking a chocolate cake. Grandy was sitting at the table, while Grandma was finishing making the icing; he kept taking fingerfuls of it, and she was scolding him. I could practically taste the cake, but that might have been because I followed *Stand Up and Speak Out!*'s advice and hadn't eaten any supper.

It felt so good being there with Grandma and Grandy and that chocolate cake that I almost didn't notice when Mr. Sanchez called for our attention.

"Students, I'm very pleased to welcome you here," he said to all of us. "I'm Mr. Sanchez, and I'll be master of ceremonies tonight. Now if you'd please line up as I call out your school name."

And he started going over all the different junior highs in the county. There were eighteen of us, and since he read them in alphabetical order, I was close to the end.

"Now count off by ones," he said, so we all did. I was number thirteen, but I was too scared to be superstitious.

"All right," he said. "That's the order you'll be reading in. Now I'm sure you all know the rules, but here's a little refresher for you. You are each to read your composition, loud and clear. The way you read your composition will count for fifty percent of your grading; the other fifty percent will be for the written work. Try to stick as closely as you can to what you wrote; the judges have received copies of each of your essays, so they'll know when you're straying. Pay attention, so you'll know when you're supposed to go onstage. Try not to talk backstage, since we don't want our speakers to be distracted. And best of luck to all of you."

The girl who'd been crying had stopped, but there was one boy who was looking pale green. I just hoped he wouldn't throw up on me.

It was time to jiggle. I sighed. I didn't want everybody thinking I was crazy, but that would be better than freezing onstage. Mr. Sanchez had already gone out and was asking everybody to stand up for "The Star-Spangled Banner." I knew I shouldn't jiggle until the song was finished, but it did make me think of the Gettysburg Address. In two weeks, I'd almost completely forgotten it. But I knew my speech really well.

When the song was finished, I started jiggling. First I rotated my head around, then I pumped my shoulders, and then I jiggled my arms and flexed my fingers, and then I started breathing deeply and jiggling my legs and wiggling my toes. By the time I was finished I didn't care if the whole world was watching. There's nothing like a good jiggle to make your body feel like conquering the world.

"You look like a runner," one of the girls whispered to me. "I see them do that before races sometimes."

"It's a relaxation technique," I said. "A psychologist taught it to me."

"You went to a psychologist for this?" the girl asked.

I nodded.

"Wow," she said. "I wish I had."

That made me feel a lot better. I didn't even want to be in Grandma's kitchen anymore. I wanted to be onstage, showing off everything I'd learned during the past two weeks.

I listened to the first few kids when they read their speeches, but after about five or six, I grew antsy and couldn't pay attention anymore. So I went back to jiggling, to keep myself loose. A couple of the other kids joined me. We looked pretty funny all jiggling together, but I felt good knowing I was showing them how to do it. For the most part the kids there looked older than me, but I was definitely the jiggling expert.

Norton Junior High was the one before Parks, so when the boy from Norton walked onstage, I walked over to the edge, so I could see him and get ready to go on. For all the jiggling, my heart was still beating pretty fast, and I was starting to pant.

So I took deep breaths and held them for a count of ten, even though it drove me crazy to do it, and then I exhaled nice and slow. It helped a lot. My heartbeat slowed down, and even though I thought I might die if I didn't go to the bathroom, I was just about positive I'd be okay. And that was the trick, of course: knowing you could do it.

"And now, representing Parks Junior High School is Miss Reesa Nathan," Mr. Sanchez said, and I found my legs were carrying me onstage.

I had to blink a couple of times because the lights were so much brighter than I'd expected. But I found my way to the lectern. My lips were dry, so I ran my tongue over them, and I cleared my throat, and then in a moment of panic I thought I'd left my speech behind, but I looked down and saw I was holding it tightly. So I put it on the lectern, where I could look down and read it easily.

I looked around the audience, and I saw my family

sitting in three chairs by the aisle. Heather was sitting with some kids from my class; I could see Ms. O'Neill with them and Mrs. Perkins. And way in the back I could make out Dr. Marks. I smiled to know she had come.

The audience was starting to rustle, and I knew that meant I should start reading. I looked down at my speech, to remind me how it started, and I took one final deep breath, and then I tried to speak.

Nothing came out.

All of a sudden I flashed onto how it had been on Monday, the panic and not being able to say a simple line, and I knew that was how it was going to be. I almost started crying, I was so mad. It wasn't fair, after all the work I'd done, to freeze just like nothing had changed.

But then I remembered what *Stand Up and Speak Out!* had said to do. "Find a friendly face and just start talking to that one person." So I looked for my mother, who has the friendliest face I know.

But I made eye contact with Robby instead. She was only three rows away, and our eyes locked. I must have looked really panicked, because she sneered at me and then she acted like she was throwing up.

That did it. "I've always known I was lucky to be born an American," I shouted out. I said it real fast, too fast, I knew, but it felt so good to have it come out right. "Although my grandparents were born in the United States, their parents weren't, and they've told me many stories of how life was in the old country, and why it was so important for them to leave and seek out a new life in the

United States." I paused for a moment and turned my face a little, so I was making eye contact with the other side of the auditorium. It was pretty easy once you got started.

"They didn't have much money, and they had to work very hard and live in tenements, but they never regretted leaving. Because they left so they'd have a chance to live a life of freedom. America offered them that chance, just as it offers that chance to Soviet defectors and Cuban refugees today. The United States offers those people the same chance as it offered my great-grandparents. The chance to live in a country that may not be perfect, but is willing to try and improve. The chance to own your own house and send your kids to good public schools and colleges. The chance to elect your presidents and senators and mayors."

Only then I realized that that wasn't what I wanted to say anymore. Maybe it had been when I wrote the composition ages back, but now I wanted to say something different. So I thought real hard while I was reading about colleges and presidents, and I decided I wasn't going to win the contest anyway, because I'd been reading too fast, and I'd started kind of weirdly. So I might as well say what I wanted to say.

"But the best chance the United States offers is the chance to change yourself," I said. I guess everybody could tell I wasn't reading anymore, since my voice was different, and I wasn't looking down at the paper anymore. "It's like Franklin Roosevelt. He had a good life and he was an important person, but then he got polio, and he couldn't really walk anymore. And he could have just retired, and not done anything more. But the United States gave him the chance to make something more out of himself, even though he was crippled. And he took that chance and he became president of the United States and he taught us that we have nothing to fear but fear itself."

I wasn't sure this was all coming out just the way I wanted it to, but there was no way of stopping myself. "The United States is a young country and I like that because I'm young too," I said. "And because we're both young, we can both change. Sometimes it's really easy to change, and sometimes it hurts. But we can grow together, and become strong and whole, and learn not to be afraid of anything. Not even of fear." I paused for a moment, and then realized I didn't have anything else to say, so I just said, "Thank you."

Everybody clapped, and for the most part I could tell they were just being polite. But then I could see Dad and Mom and Robby stand up and clap really wildly, and then Ms. O'Neill and my classmates were all cheering, even though Mr. Sanchez had told the audience not to cheer, and Dr. Marks was standing up too, making a victory sign with her hand held up high, and I knew I'd better get off the stage real fast, because I was going to start crying. So I walked as fast as I could, and then as soon as I got offstage, and the next kid was introduced, I started shaking and shaking, and then I was laughing a little and crying. I didn't care what anybody else thought. I'd done it. I'D DONE IT!!! It was over, and I'd done it. And it felt so good.

Mr. Sanchez read off the winners, and sure enough I hadn't won. There was no way I was going to. We were all onstage then, and we clapped along with the audience when the winners were announced. I felt like a runner-up in the Miss America contest. But that was okay too. I'd won what I wanted to win.

Then they drew the curtain, and we could leave. I got my stuff together, walked down the stairs by the side of the stage, and joined my family.

"We're so proud of you," Dad said and hugged me. Mom hugged me too. Even Robby looked proud.

"Did you see what I did to help you?" she asked me.

"That was supposed to help me?" I asked.

"It got you going," she said. "I could see you were just standing there getting ready to freeze."

"I would have gotten started without you," I said, but then I knew that it didn't matter. So I hugged Robby too.

All my classmates came over then, and Dr. Marks joined us, and I was busy introducing everybody and hearing their congratulations. Ms. O'Neill had tears in her eyes, and she admitted she'd cried when I finished. So I admitted I had too.

"But you know something," I said, realizing it just then. "It was kind of fun."

"Really?" Heather asked.

"Yeah," I said. "Sort of like seeing a scary movie. Once I got started, I enjoyed it."

"That's great," Dr. Marks said. "I think it's safe to say that's one phobia that's bit the dust."

"Hey, Ms. O'Neill," I said. "Didn't you say something about the junior high play having auditions soon?"

"Next week," she said. "Oh, Reesa—do you really think you're ready?"

"Well, I didn't win the contest," I said. "But I feel a winning streak coming on!"

MS READ-a-thon— a simple way to start youngsters reading

Boys and girls between 6 and 14 can join the MS READ-a-thon and help find a cure for Multiple Sclerosis by reading books. And they get two rewards — the enjoyment of reading, and the great feeling that comes from helping others.

Parents and educators: For complete information call your local MS chapter. Or mail the coupon below.

Kids can help, too!

- - - - - - - - - - - - - - - - - -

Mail to:
National Multiple Sclerosis Society
205 East 42nd Street
New York, N.Y. 10017
I would like more information about the MS READ-a-thon and how it can work in my area.

Name_____
(please print)
Address_____
City_____ State_____ Zip_____
Organization_____

1—80